Dog

Food

Raynesha Pittman

Write 2 Eat Concepts Presents:
Dog Food

For information contact: Write2Eat2@gmail.com

ISBN: 978-0982492079
LCCN: TBD

Editing: www.21StreetUrbanEditing.com
Typesetting: 21StreetUrbanEditing.com

Chapter One:
Change Is Coming

It's been said that if you're looking for new beginnings, seek them through God, because He specializes in creating them. If that shit's true then the change was my mama. She was constantly on her hands and knees. Either her prayers fell upon deaf ears, or she had been praying to the wrong muthafucka. Change came, but it came at the expense of my happiness and freedom. I guess it fucked my mama up, too. If I would've known her prayers would one day come true, I would've been sending up counteracting prayers to block her shit. Like one of them deep-south, *Roots*-believing-in niggas, I could feel it in my soul when her prayers had been answered. From the time the nipple-hardening, cold air hit my shirtless body after she snatched the covers off me, I knew something wasn't right. Fuck that. I knew at that moment shit would never be right again.

"Wake up, mister. It's time to rise 'n shine and give God all the glory."

My mama's morning greetings normally shielded off everything that stopped my daily

1

progress. Being sleepy or cold would never outweigh her display of love for me, but that particular morning, she had to step her game up and come harder.

"Good morning, God. Good morning, Mama. I need thirty more minutes of sleep. And why is it so cold in here? You didn't forget to pay the heat bill, did you?"

I snatched the covers right back out of her hands, wrestled with them until I was nice and snug, and then headed back to sleep like my mama was a chump.

"Thank you Jesus. You are worthy to be King! You touched my womb a little over thirteen years ago and said I was worthy to bring life into this world. You showed a lost soul like mine unconditional love, who has always paid all her bills on time, might I add! I'm sure you won't mind if I snatch his little sleepy tail up by the flesh and beat him 'till he's black and blue. Boy, if you don't get your butt up out this bed I'm gon'—"

There was no way I was going to let her finish that sentence.

"Okay, Mama. I'm up!" I threw the covers off my body and placed both feet on the floor so there would be no seconding guessing if I was awake.

"I thought you'd see it my way," she giggled, but the attitude still lingered in her voice. "You got thirty minutes to have yourself dressed and ready for breakfast before we leave out for church. Not a minute later, Demarcus. Do you hear me?"

"Yes ma'am, I hear you. Thirty minutes, not a minute more!"

As she turned around to exit my room, I could hear her mumbling all kinds of un-Christian like words underneath her breath. "I pay all my damn bills on time! That boy better get his ass together and stop playing with me! Gon' sit up in my face and say did I forget to pay the heat? He done lost his damn mind."

"Mama!" I had to stop her before she made it down the hallway to the kitchen and her attitude turned that good ol' bacon, eggs, grits and toast she cooked every Sunday into a bowl of cereal with a can of condensed milk.

"What now, boy?"

"I love you."

She looked me in my eyes and I watched the anger disappear. With that same sweeter-than-sugar alto voice she had originally greeted me with she said, "I love you too, baby. This mama pays all her bills on time! Now get yo' tail ready for church while I cook you this breakfast. You gon' make me burn the bread!"

"Yes ma'am."

I stretched, yawned, and relieved the gas that had been dancing around my stomach all night from the cabbage she had cooked the night before. It's funny how her threats of whooping my butt always gave me the energy I thought I lacked. I headed to the closet to find something to wear quickly. I wasn't that fond of church, but it was my mama's thing. Every Sunday and Wednesday we were there like clockwork. Mama, aka Sister Sharon, was in the choir on the usher board and doing anything else that allowed her to keep her mind off of a man and her focus locked on me and the Lord. There were times when we'd spend five days out of the week there because her duties called. I never complained about going, because I knew nothing I could say would make that woman change her mind about me putting the Lord first. I couldn't even take the trash out without mama making me give thanks for being healthy enough to complete the chore. She even forced me to pay my tithes out the allowance I earned, making me the first and only kid at the church to do so.

The church we attended was run by her uncle, Pastor Leroy Elder of First Missionary Baptist Church of Westwood. He was the most talked about pastor in all of Memphis, because those who knew or knew of Pastor Leroy before he got saved knew him as the pimping, drug dealing and shit-starting Leroy. I won't knock the man for getting saved. He needed to, but I just wished the saving was visible both inside and out. Uncle Leroy, as we called him, pulled up to church every

Dog Food

Sunday in a different color Cadillac. The dates of his 'Lacs ranged from the early 1970s to this year's 1995 Cadillac Deville. All of them were on four whitewall tires. There wasn't anything wrong with him still loving Caddies. Where he fucked up was pulling into the church's parking lot blasting David Ruffin, Rick James or Al Green in his rides. Picture trying to praise the Lord with *Super Freak* stuck in your head because the pastor had it playing on blast before the service.

Unc still looked like a pimp, too. He would step out the 'Lac dressed in multicolored, double-breasted silk suits with snakeskin loafers on his feet. Every week he had a different pretty young thang on the passenger side that he always claimed to be helping to get saved. The man killed me with his oversized cowboy hats tilted to the right, causing the brim to touch his animal fur shoulder throw that he left open to show off his nappy chest hairs and many gold chains. He came to church looking like he was fresh off the ho stroll, and he still preached his sermons. The nigga rocked a full-teeth smile to show off his two gold fangs at the top of his mouth that he loved to pick at with his ex-cocaine snorting pinky finger. His pinky nail had to be at least an inch and a half long, and he kept it manicured. It was always hard to determine if I was being blinded by his fangs or the extra-large rock that sat on a twenty-four-carat gold band he had iced out on his pinky.

The dude was cold with it, and as good as his words were when he was convincing women to sell their heads and tails for him, he was just as encouraging with his words on the pulpit. I've seen Unc cause people to cry and pass out.

His biggest trick happened once when he caused a few members to get the Holy Ghost. When the Spirit was flowing, he made sure the dough was too. He was so smooth with it that this offering didn't even have a name to it. He waited until the room was all rattled up then gave his ushers a look that said, *Go get that money, ho!* They got the baskets floating around with no questions asked.

But seriously, Unc was an inspiration for all of Memphis' lost souls aiming to be saints. With his team of deacons who were pimps, drug dealers, and mack daddies, he gave sinners hopes of new beginnings. And that's why my mama never missed a beat. Yeah, I lied and told people we went to church there because it was our uncle's church, but the truth was, my mama had a past before she found out she was pregnant with me. This church is what helped her change. In her words, she used to be addicted to sinning with men who kept their pockets fat. You'd think with skin as dark and smooth as hers, with not a blemish in sight and a rump similar to a donkey's, it should've been the men sinning over her. But her sister, Auntie Cat, had a version of my mama's past that was a hell of a lot different.

****

"While yo' mama spends all her time down talking me and Uncle Leroy, she didn't tell you how she use to suck dick for dollars, did she? A ho is a ho, and even though yo' mama called herself being a pimp's woman, she wasn't nothing more than a bottom bitch. Now go run yo' little bitch ass off and tell her what I said!"

I never asked my mama, because I hated my Auntie Cat and the jerk-ass nigga she gave birth to. I knew my auntie and cousin, Little Omar, were jealous of us, even though they really didn't have a reason to be. My aunt was a young girl when she hooked up with a light-skinned nigga named Big Omar from Mississippi. He sold crack and was proud of it. He wasn't her husband, just my cousin's dad, and he made sure neither one of them wanted for anything. The money he made was rolling in good, so my auntie quit her day job of TV watching and weed smoking to join in on the action. Now my cousin had not only one drug dealer funding his future; he had two.

If anybody should've been jealous, it should've been us. They had a little happy family with a mama, a daddy, and a son. We didn't have shit. My daddy bounced before my mama had given birth to me, and everything we ever had took my mama's blood, sweat and tears to get. She worked ten hour days as an RN for a nursing home just to make ends meet. My aunt sat on her fat ass serving fiends all day and night, and then she had the nerve to complain about being tired. I wished my father had been around to go work all them fucked up hours leaving my mama at the house to tend to me, but I knew it would never happen.

Anytime I got the nerve to ask about my father, my mama always cut me off quickly by saying, "Stop worrying about the devil before the devil starts worrying about you!" I didn't know what the hell she was talking about, but I knew to let it go.

****

When I hopped out of the tub, I could hear my mama yelling back and forth with somebody in the kitchen, so I threw on my slacks quickly and headed to see what the problem was.

"I know that's your sister, Sharon, but the bitch is stupid. I told my baby sister on the day she pushed the ho out she'd brought another dumb bitch into this world. Everybody cussed me out about it, but I was right!"

I heard the sound of a lighter flicked multiple times like the fluid in it was too low to ignite, and then I heard the sound of my uncle inhaling deeply. Between coughing and exhaling, he managed to finish.

Dog Food

"Look at the bullshit she done got herself into. Now she wants us to help get her ass out of it, and for free! I ain't never worked a day in my life for free!"

"You ain't never worked a day in your life, and I told you not to smoke that shit in my house, Leroy. You know Demarcus is here!"

Uncle Leroy took two or three more quick puffs of his joint and then put it out so my mama could continue.

"I agree with you when it comes to Catherine, but she's still family. If our help can keep her out of jail or from ending up in a casket, then we need to do our part. Shit, I done burnt the toast fooling with you!"

I could hear my mama moving about the kitchen swiftly. Then, the all-too-familiar sound of the butter knife scrapping the burnt layer off the toast filled the room.

"I'm calling on you to help me help her, Leroy. I know y'all ain't ever gotten along. Hell, me and Cat ain't ever gotten along either, but we family, and we is all we got left."

"But I told that bitch years ago when she started craving money that I could help her ass out and give her a job. But naw, everybody wanted to say Unc was wrong when all I was trying to do was look out—"

My mama cut him off in mid-sentence, "All you were trying to do is put your own flesh and blood on the corner with a price tag while you got a large percent of the money. I can't believe you fixed your mouth to ask your youngest niece to ho for you and even took her down to the stroll! Now you try to justify it as looking out for your family. You better pray that the Lord forgave you for that."

My uncle placed both elbows on the kitchen table and leaned in closer to mama.

"While you sitting over there hoping the Lord forgave me, you better pray all that pussy you was givin' them pimps was forgiven too. Since you want to bring up the past, who's Dee's daddy anyway? You shonuff didn't get pregnant by the Lord! You love to talk about other people's mistakes, but don't forget, she ain't the only one I took to the stroll in this family. She's just the only ho in this family who said no!"

"You dirty muthafucka! I was young and dumb back then and thought I could trust my dog-ass uncle. Don't think I don't know you're using the church's walls to sell pussy. You think you're slick using them ignorant bitches to sell pussy in the name of the Lord. You might have your congregation fooled, but I know you. You weren't shit then and you ain't shit now. Don't you bring yo' nothing ass in my house and try—"

Uncle Leroy interrupted Mama by obnoxiously clearing his throat as he watched me standing in the hallway listening.

Dog Food

"Boy, what are you doing standing in the hallway like a damn coat rack listening to grown folks talk? Come on over here and give your favorite uncle a handshake, Dee. I told you about trying to grow up before your time. It's bad enough yo' mama treats you like her man when she needs to go out and get her one!"

"I don't need a man, Leroy," she said, irritated.

The nigga wasn't my favorite uncle; he was my only uncle. I shook his hand quickly and then hurried to my seat at the kitchen table. The lingering smell of weed and his loud-ass cologne was making me lose my appetite. We ate in silence like we always did because the food was too good to spoil with meaningless conversation. When we all were done, I started cleaning off the table as my chores instructed me to, but mama sent me off with words I never thought I'd hear come out of her mouth.

"I'll clean off the table, baby. You go take them good clothes off and put on something else. We won't be attending church today."

The joy of knowing I didn't have to sit in church all day sent me running down the hall to change. I was just about to fly in my room when I heard the words that would cause a young mind like mine to fall into a state of curiosity. It's like Unc had said it loud and clear to make sure I heard it.

"Fucking with that Dog Food just got your sister sized up for a body bag. How are we supposed to help?"

Chapter Two:
Watch Yo' Mouth

"What's Dog Food?" I knew I couldn't ask my mama or uncle; they would've told me to stay in child's place. So I asked the only nigga around my age that would know.

"What's Dog Food? Nigga, are you serious?" Little Omar had his right arm extended at the old oak tree with his invisible gun in hand, pretending to shoot the birds in the nest. "Pow, pow, pow! Die little bitches."

I waited until he put his imaginary gun away, not wanting to be the next victim on his killing spree before I asked again. "So, are you going to tell me or what?"

"Damn nigga. My mama said you were slow, but I didn't think you were that damn stupid!"

I hated when he quoted his mama's negative thoughts about me. That's why I didn't want to ask his ass shit, but the way the adults rushed us out of the house when he and his parents arrived, I had to know what Dog Food was.

"I'm not stupid! I just want to know what dog food is, and I know you know."

"'I'm not stupid,'" he said in a voice that was supposed to sound like mine. "Damn, y'all kids these days need guidance. But I forgot you don't have a daddy and yo' mama a stuck-up square, so you probably don't know. It's smack, young nigga."

"Smack?"

"Smack, nigga! H, Hero, Chocolate, Boy, Horse…"

He kept shooting off names, and with each one I became more confused. He acted like his fifteen years on this earth were a century ahead of my thirteen years because he knew a little more about the streets than me. He must've forgotten that for only fifteen-years old, he had been exposed to a lot of shit thirty and forty-year olds hadn't even witnessed. He was kidnapped at six and held for ransom, which turned out to be about small amount of cocaine. I remember his mama bragging about how her little solider could cook, weigh and bag cocaine at eight. By age ten, he was arrested with his father for beating up a buyer who had tried to run off with their stash. Comparing his first ten years of life to mine, anybody would realize that a childhood was missing from his.

By the way he wore his life on his face, you'd think the nigga was eighteen or twenty. He had permanent bruises from head to toe and his eyes looked like they belonged to a man in his late sixties, because they were sunk in and ringed up. Although people assumed we were brothers because we both had midnight-toned skin, round faces, hazel eyes, and identical full lips, our noses begged to differ. I had our family's big, round nose. He took after his daddy's nose which was long and pointy. When we were younger, I had taken pride in knowing I had a twin in this world, but now I saw it as more of a curse. When I looked at him, my body filled with hatred because of the way he treated me. A part of me felt like hating him meant hating myself. The nigga was my evil twin, and for some fucked up reason, it seemed like evil always prevailed.

"Look Omar, I don't know what any of that means, so if you think I'm dumb, explain it to me like you're speaking to a dummy then."

"It's heroin. H-E-R-O-I-N. Now you get it, dumb-ass nigga?"

"Yeah, I get it, jerk. But that's all you had to say in the first place."

"Don't try to get smart, dumb ass nigga," he said, taking a step closer to me. "I didn't have to tell your soft ass shit. And why you want to know, anyway?"

"Because I know that's what they're in the house talking about. Something to do with your mama and heroin–" When the word heroin came out my mouth, he shot me a look of death, so I hurriedly corrected myself.

"I mean Dog Food."

"You don't know shit, so you shouldn't be saying shit," he spat. "Why are you and yo' mama so fuckin' nosey?"

"We ain't nosey. We trying to help y'all fix the problem. Whatever that is..."

"We don't need y'all help! How some pussy bitches gon' help us? We came over here so I can stay a couple of days while my daddy straightens shit out. We don't need y'all help!"

It wasn't the right time to ask, but he was so emotional and on the brink of tears, so I threw it out there.

"What happened, twin?"

It was a weak attempt at a truce, but it worked. He began telling me how he wasn't supposed to know what was going on, but he had overheard his parents arguing one night. His daddy hooked up with some guys from the north that had a killer deal on some heroin. From what he said, the money from cocaine was crumbs compared to the money you can make selling *Dog Food*, so his daddy went all in. But, what his daddy didn't expect was for Auntie Cat to get a table habit from handling it. She got all diabetic over the shit and started shooting it up.

"Man, that shit got my mama strung out. She doesn't even eat anymore. That's why her ass is so skinny now!"

Dog Food

It had been months since I'd seen my aunt, so her being skinny sounded like a lie, but I wasn't going to contest it. I was too scared that he would stop talking. He continued to tell me how his mama had gotten a hold of his daddy's stash. When it was time to pay out the niggas from up north, the money was short. He said the supplier gave them a week to get their money right, but that was after he forced Big Omar to watch as he forced Auntie Cat to suck his dick at gunpoint.

"My daddy ain't no bitch, and the nigga had violated my mama, so he waited until the nigga tucked his gun away before he snatched the nigga off the ground by his neck and choked him to death. I don't know what he did with the body, but like two days later, all these random niggas from Detroit started popping up asking for their brother's whereabouts, so we got low on their asses."

"Then what happened?"

He had me hype like I was listening to a hood bedtime story. The shit he was telling me was only heard of in books that I wasn't old enough to read yet. Never in a million years would my mama approve of me hearing how ratchet the drug world was. I was intrigued by it.

"Nothing happened. Well, not yet. Today is my parent's normal day to re-up, and my daddy said if they don't go, it will cause suspicion and speculation, so they gotta go. Ain't nothing going to happen to them. He's just paranoid that they're going to look at my mama and tell she's been shooting up, so he wants to play it safe. But we're good!"

Little Omar's voice held too much confidence in it. I don't think he really understood what his parents had gotten themselves caught up in. I didn't understand it either, but from what I had heard my uncle say earlier, it was dangerous.

"Y'all not good! Something bad is about to go down."

"Aye, you better watch your mouth, ho. Ain't shit bad about to go down, nigga!"

"Yes it is. Yo' mama about to be in a body bag." I didn't think before I said it, nor did I share with him that those were our uncle's words.

The words just flew out of my mouth like hot lava erupting from a volcano. His fist met my face backed by that same type of power. He threw one punch after another, catching me several times in my mouth, nose and left eye. The heat from my temper mixed with the blood, snot and tears sent a preview of the taste of death to my lips. I could feel my left eye closing to the rhythm of my racing heartbeat until it was closed shut. As his uppercut missed its target and only grazed my chin, I took advantage of the opportunity. I threw my hands up, cupped the blood leaking from my nose, and took off running like a track star.

Dog Food

"Mama! Help me! Omar is trying to kill me!" I ran up the porch steps two at a time, and before I could grab the rusted knob on the screen door, my mama was headed out of it with all the adults following her. She bypassed me, but she took a quick eyeshot of my injuries and went straight for my cousin.

"I know I've told you to keep your hands off my son, Little Omar," she said with a handful of Omar's once nicely pressed, blue, button-down shirt balled in her hand.

"Let me go, bitch! You ain't my mama."

I'm glad I hadn't blinked or I would have missed my mama slapping the black off his face. "You disrespectful son of a bitch! There's no way I'm letting this raggedy-ass child of yours spend one night in my house!"

"Fuck you, Sharon! Ain't nothing raggedy but the pussy and the sorry-ass nigga that bred this little bitch," Auntie Cat yelled in retaliation as she snatched me up by my shirt.

"You're always so quick to blame Little Omar for their fights when he wouldn't have to whoop Dee's ass if he wasn't such a faggot! He ain't a mama's boy. You just gave birth to a daughter with a dick."

They went back and forth, insulting each other's' child until my uncle Leroy and Big Omar got involved in the dispute. They got the women to release our shirts and then pushed us out of harm's way.

I was fascinated at how much weight Auntie Cat had lost, but what really had my full attention was the nasty needle-mark rashes she had in the cracks of her arms. I was off to the side, staring at them in both curiosity and disgust until my mama's words to her sister snapped me out of it.

"You, Brillo-pad-arm-resembling bitch! Get your junky ass off my property and take both of your criminals with you. Don't come by here again, and if you see me in the streets don't speak, because I don't have no intentions of seeing none of you bitches until your funerals. Good day!"

And that's exactly what happened. Three days after my mama cleared out her yard and shipped Little Omar off with Uncle Leroy and Auntie Cat, we were notified that their nude bodies were recovered from the Mississippi River.

Damn!

Chapter Three:
Lost Souls

Change showed its ass in the days following the funerals. Uncle Leroy was arrested for ties in a prostitution ring. His face was on the front of every newspaper in the city. The newspaper headlines ranged from *Pimping Preachers* to *He Put the H-O In Holy*. The media was having a ball exposing Uncle Leroy's dirty laundry, especially when they found out he was related to the Jane Doe found floating in the Mississippi River. This was the same person for whom he had received his prior conviction. I don't think the media realized how influencing their propaganda would be, because thanks to them, Uncle Leroy was listed as a suspect in Auntie Cat's and Big Omar's murders.

It wasn't a secret that none of our family got along, nor was it a secret that after my grandmother died and left Uncle Leroy in charge of her two girls, he had gotten them caught up in bad lifestyles. Although Auntie Cat was smart enough to decline his offer, she made sure to tell everyone she knew, including her school teachers, how he had tried to solicit her. Since Auntie Cat was sixteen when it happened, the school jumped all over it. Uncle Leroy went to jail. That's where the hatred between the two of them started. Now that it was public information that Unc was back in the pimping game, my aunt's mysterious murder smelled like it had something to do with him.

Little Omar, who now wanted to be called *Omar* or *Big O* because he planned on living his father's legacy, knew whoever had a hand in his parents murder. However, he refused to tell the authorities what he knew to clear Uncle Leroy's name. He was on his renegade shit, vowing to avenge his parents' death, even if it meant his own. I expected for him to take their deaths hard, which he did, but I can't say that it caused him to change. He started selling drugs full-time, skipping school, and smoking weed like he was into lawn and gardening. He was already on that path before they died. Their deaths only enhanced the inevitable by giving it a jumpstart.

Omar moved in with us after his parents were murdered. You'd think he'd be humble for my mama moving him in and not letting him get trapped in the system, but that would be too close to right. Omar's hate for me and my mama intensified, and he didn't give a damn about showing it. His bullying of me turned into endless days and nights of torture. I had no choice but to deal with it, because when change came, it took my mama's soul during the process.

Dog Food

As fucked up as it may sound, the truth still remained that my mama wished death upon her sister. She was angry, but she would never forgive herself for the heated words she spoke to Aunt Cat that sent her to her casket. Her sorrow over what and how things happened messed her up for good. I thought time would heal her, but it never did. She started drinking heavily just to function. I watched it go from a cup or two at the repast to her stashing a never-ending bottle in the refrigerator. That bottle turned into two, then three. Eventually, her liquor found a new spot next to her bed. It wasn't long before my mama needed a drink before and after work. I wouldn't be surprised if she drank at work. She started chain smoking cigarettes, and when that wasn't enough to ease her mind, she'd roll her up a joint and take it to the head. Her going to church became a thing of the past. There were more men coming in and out of our house pretending to be my daddy than the law allowed.

I didn't say anything to her about it until I turned sixteen and she decided to move in her man, Lamont. Although I had known Lamont all my life since he worked with my mama at the nursing home, I wasn't trying to have the nigga as my step-daddy. It was too late to push a man into my life. She got the chance to see it for herself, firsthand.

"Demarcus, wake yo' ass up! Lamont is taking you to do some yard work with him today. When you get paid, buy me a pack of cigarettes. I'll pay you back on Friday."

"Man Mama, I'm not about to work on yards with Lamont. I got to ice my knees and get ready for tonight's game. How am I going to be the biggest running back to ever come out of Tennessee if I'm pushing a lawnmower with a broke ass male nurse?"

She laughed as she reminisced about the plans I told her I had for my future.

"I guess you can't go, because you owe me a brand new house and Lexus mister big time football player and mass communications major," she said while exhaling smoke. "Well, I'll go tell Lamont's no-degree-havin' ass that you ain't going with him. I'll make that nigga buy my smokes."

"Thanks Mom-duce, I love you."

I could smell the weed smoke coming from down the hallway, which meant Omar was up. He was eighteen now and owned his own car. If I offered the right amount of gas money, he'd take me to get my ice. I knocked on his bedroom door.

"If you ain't a female, smoking on that Bill Clinton presidential shit, or talking money, get the fuck away from my door."

Dog Food

He turned up Master P's, *Make Em' Say Uhh* to block out the sound of my knocks, so I just walked in.

"Didn't I tell you don't come in my shit without an invitation?"

"Save it! You come in my room waking me up every morning on some bullshit without an invitation," I shot back.

"Yo' mama gave me authority over you, little nigga, when she made it my job to make sure you get to school on time. Run up in my shit without permission again and I'm gon' pop yo' little ass."

He lifted his shirt with one hand to flash his gun and with the other he continued smoking green.

"You don't wake me up; you beat me until I get up, and if you so grown and got all this authority, why are you still living with us? You're *Big O*, the next big timer in the streets next to Lord King's old ass. Don't tell me you're his right hand man, putting in all the work, and he's keeping all the money?"

He jumped to his feet. "I got money, broke-ass nigga." He moved to his bedroom door and locked it. Then he dashed to his closet floor. "I know how much I got. You the only nigga who knows where my stash is, so if anything comes up missing, you're a dead man!"

He pulled up a piece of his closet's floor and snatched out a small army-style duffle bag from the shallow hole he had dug underneath the house. As I looked closer, I noticed that Omar had dug himself an entrance in and out the house. He saw me looking at it.

"That's my emergency exit just in case shit hits the fan," he said, emptying the contents of the bag onto his bed. There were different-sized sandwich bag bundles wrapped in rubber bands. He had two Ziploc bags full of weed. The bigger bag was full of dark green weed; it looked almost brownish. The smaller one was filled with lime-green-colored weed, which I assumed was his smoke stash. There were three shoebox-sized items wrapped in brown paper bags, another gun much bigger than the one he was carrying, and more cash than I'd ever seen in my life.

"Who broke now, bitch?" He laughed like he was on some type of boss shit with an evil villain smile on his face. I noticed he had a band aid under his eye, but he was always fighting, so I didn't bother asking what had happened.

"Then go buy your balling ass a house then and get the fuck out of ours!" Envy was present in my voice.

"Naw ho. I'ma keep stacking until I have enough money to buy this bitch right here. Then I'ma put you and your mama's asses out in the street and turn your room into my private strip club."

Dog Food

He wasn't getting our house, but I knew why he wanted it. We lived on a dead-end street named Bluebell Cove which had great access to the hood, meaning more drug sales. But his dream wasn't happening, because my mama had already told me how when she went to glory the house would be mine.

"Sorry to kill your dreams of jacking your dick in my room, but this is going to be my house and I ain't selling it!"

"Shut up nigga, you don't hear that?" Omar asked, turning down his CD player.

"Sound like yo' mama and that bitch-ass nigga Lamont in there getting them up."

I stood still for a moment, and then I heard the arguing. My mama was laying into his ass, but I wanted to know for what. I headed out of Omar's room and Omar's nosey ass was right behind me. When we got to my mother's door, Omar blocked it so I couldn't go in.

"They're grown, little nigga. Let them argue that shit out."

I wanted to protest, but listening to the words being yelled became more of importance.

"Yeah, I called yo' son a mama's boy! You've babied his ass all of his life and now he's a little bitch. He don't do shit around here but wash dishes and clean off the table. Those ain't boy chores."

At the sound of him calling me out my name, I tried to push past Omar, but he wouldn't move.

"You can't get mad because the nigga's telling yo' mama the truth. I've been calling you a little bitch all of your life. It's time yo' mama heard it from somebody else."

"Fuck you! I ain't no bitch!"

"Then why are you sitting here with tears welling in your eyes, nigga?"

"You're the only little bitch I know, Lamont."

My mama's words stopped me from responding to Omar.

Then, the sound of a slap and thud sent me and Omar running into the room. When we busted into the room, my mother was on the floor holding the right side of her face, and Lamont was hovering over her with his chest heaving up and down. The shit felt like one of those old school, black-and-white movies where the scenes jumped from scene to scene due to fucked up film. First, we were at the door, then Omar was beating Lamont's ass, and the last scene was Omar and I stomping his ass out.

I was surprised that my mama didn't try to stop us, but when we were done she looked at Lamont. "Get yo' shit and get the fuck out of my house, bitch!"

Chapter Four:
From Boy to Man

Going in on Lamont with Omar seemed to bring us closer together for the first time in our lives. He still made his little fucked-up comments to me every now and then, but he wouldn't be Little O if he didn't. As my high school graduation passed and my eighteenth birthday approached, the nigga seemed more excited about it than me.

"Damn, little nigga. In two weeks your ass is about to be a grown-ass virgin. I still can't believe you're on your way to play running back for the Crimson Tide. I hate to say it, but nigga you did that shit! With over two thousand rushing yards last season, Auburn, LSU, and the Vols ain't ready for you. You like the next Barry Sanders around this bitch."

My mouth dropped in shock of Omar knowing my stats. I didn't think he paid that much attention. I mean, he came to a few of my games as a senior, but he never complimented me on my performances before.

"Close yo' mouth before I find something to put in it! Yeah, I keep up with yo' ass. You know a nigga really like your daddy the way I schooled you to life." He laughed.

"Nigga, you ain't been nothing like my daddy, but I appreciate you giving me my props. And I ain't a virgin. If you don't believe me, ask your bitch."

"Which one you talking about, ho? But for real though, we kicking it tough, for your one-eight. If yo' little ass act right, I just might let you lose your virginity to one of my bitches."

"Whatever nigga."

For the first time since change had come into my life, everything was going good. My mom had gotten a job in the emergency room at Methodist Central Hospital, and her drinking had stopped. I couldn't get her to kick her cigarette smoking, but at least she was back in church. Our relationship had gotten back to the way it was when I was younger, but that might've been because we never saw each other anymore. She was at the hospital for what seemed like days. With college approaching and my football career jumping off, I had been in and out the house for days at a time myself. We didn't even have time to celebrate my birthday together. We had a quick lunch at the hospital cafeteria, and she sang happy birthday to me with the help of a few of her nursing friends. She bought me an Alabama fitted cap and gave me a card with five hundred dollars in it, which was exactly what I needed to get me an outfit for the party Omar was throwing for me.

I hit the mall and snatched up an Alabama shirt to match my hat, a pair of dark blue, loose-fitted jeans, and some burgundy and white high top Forces to match. I wasn't flashy; I had never been the flashy type. Being five foot ten, almost two hundred pounds, and totally in shape, I didn't have to try and look good like the rest of the niggas out there. And, having hazel eyes and being the most talked about running back in the state had its advantages too.

Omar didn't know it, but he was right. I was a virgin. I had gotten some head a few times, but I'd never popped off the natural way. I wasn't saving myself for marriage or no shit like that. I just wanted my first time to be with a girl that meant something to me. But when I woke up this particular morning, I changed my mind about it. I needed to get some experience under my belt before I fucked around and lost my first love to not being able to satisfy her in the bed. If Omar really had some hos lined up for me to smash, I had a pocket full of rubbers with their names on them.

We left the house around nine and headed to Persuasion Gentlemen's club. I had heard about it from my teammates who had turned eighteen before me. The club was supposed to be the hottest strip club in Memphis and had the prettiest bitches to ever work a pole on staff. I hadn't been around to judge, but I'd say everything I'd heard about the place was true. When I walked in, all I could see was money. The entertainers looked like money and so did the guests. I always wondered where the niggas with the big pockets relaxed, and this seemed to be the place. There was so much Versace, Dolce and Gabbana and Rolex in the building, I was glad I hadn't tried to dress flashy. I couldn't compete.

It was my first time partaking in live entertainment, so Omar made sure he went all out. We had the VIP section on lock with bottles covering every table. It was full of niggas I didn't know, but they all showed me love. Omar had invited Lord King himself, and he and Omar had given me a grand apiece in one dollar bills to make it rain. Lord King purchased my first lap dance for me. I fell in love with the stripper. Her name was Silk, and it fit her to the tee. She had these long, silky legs and long hair that matched. She put my hands on her ass, and it felt like silk too. From her golden complexion to her pretty white teeth, she was perfect. What I couldn't understand while she was giving me my lap dance was why niggas paid all that money to get their dicks hard in public, knowing you couldn't bust a nut. I knew this would be my first and last time in a place like this, because every time my dick got hard I tensed up and felt embarrassed.

Dog Food

"Relax, I'm not going to bite you unless you want me to," she whispered in my ear.

"I am relaxed."

"No you're not. Every time you poke me with your hard-ass dick, you tense up. You don't have to worry; I love a big hard dick."

I almost shot off by her words alone. I'd had high school girls tell me my dick was big, but this was coming from a woman. Not just any woman, but one who men spent money on just to drool over.

"So, you're the rich, big-time running back everybody in the city has been talking about, huh?"

My answer was delayed from me debating on telling her I wasn't rich and from me taking the time to thank God for my talents on the football field. "Yeah, that's me. I got a couple of stacks in the bank." I decided to lie, because one day I would be rich.

"Well, I got a special birthday present for you once we get out of here. I promise to make you feel better than every dollar you got in the bank."

She took off her bra and a plastic card fell on my lap. She put her buxom breasts in my face as she whispered in my ear.

"Don't lose that. It's our room key. Tonight, Silk is all yours, baby."

She got off my lap as my dance came to an end. I dug in my pockets and pulled out a wad of ones. I wasn't sure how much it was, but when I tried to give her my tip, she declined.

"No boo, you keep that. I've already been paid for. Just make sure you tell Lord King and Big O thank you."

Before I could look around the VIP to find Omar, he was heading my way. "So, what did you think about your dance from the beautiful Silk?" Omar asked.

"It was cool, I guess."

"You guess? Come on now young nigga. She's one of the baddest bitches in this club."

"I said it was cool..." I leaned in closer to my big cousin and whispered, "but my dick kept getting hard."

Omar could've died from the way he was laughing. He turned to my guests.

"Somebody get the birthday boy a drink."

I was given something dark that kind of burnt my throat, but after the second one I was throwing them back. All night I was given lap dances, but none had affected me like Silk's. I didn't want another bitch to rub her shit on me; I only wanted Silk. I took the room key out of my pocket and started turning it in my hand. As the drinks kept coming, the urge to find Silk kept getting worse.

When Omar made his way back to me, he had a set of twins following him. "See, I told y'all I had a twin too. You stay with me and you..." he said

Dog Food

to the twin that wasn't as physically blessed as her sister. "Go over there and show my twin a good time."

"Naw Omar, I'm good. Where's Silk?"

"Aww, now your drunk ass is looking for Silk. She had to leave and get ready for her next performance, if you know what I mean, so let Peaches," he looked from one twin to the other then continued, "or Cream, whichever one you want, keep you occupied until it's time to bounce."

"I'm good! I'll just wait for Silk."

"You'll just wait for Silk? Aye, let me holler at you in the men's room for a minute," Omar said.

He dismissed the girls and we went to the restroom.

"Here nigga, smoke this. You need to relax! Don't get to the hotel and fall in love with that bitch. She's a ho, and you got a future ahead of you. No matter what that bitch is talking about, remember to never trust a bitch! She's looking for dollars, and your broke ass ain't got none."

I heard him, but I wasn't trying to listen. I took the blunt and hit it so we could end the conversation like Indians sharing a peace pipe. "Omar, I need to power back up. Can you take me to the hotel now? I want to get some rest before she gets there."

He gave me a fucked-up look but took me to my destination. When we got in my room, he had a blunt already on the table waiting for me, a box of condoms and a bottle of Remy. "Fuck her 'til you can't fuck no more, little cousin. And I'll be back to get you in the morning. Don't forget what I said to you in the restroom, nigga. Trust no bitch!"

He bounced to give me time to rest, but I was too drunk and excited to chill. I walked around the one-bedroom suite but realized I was in no condition to walk. I was fucked up, and everything I looked at was spinning. By the time Silk had arrived, I was halfway done with the bottle of Remy and seeing double.

"Hey boo, I thought I'd make it a night to remember, so I brought my best friend along. I hope you don't mind."

I didn't mind, because her friends were just as bad as she was but I thought she said friend. After the dark-skinned girl walked in, another beautiful, golden-skinned girl followed along behind her. I knew my vision was sending me shit in pairs, but there still were six bitches in my face instead of four. Before I could ask about the extra bodies, Silk was already making introductions through pops of her bubble gum.

"That's Coco and this is my little sister, Sierra. She'll be waiting in the room until we're done giving you your gift."

"Hi," Sierra said and then went straight to the other room, closing the door behind her.

Dog Food

Before I could make an attempt at small talk, Silk and Coco were doing their thing. Silk went straight to her knees, freed my man, and began giving me head at the door while CoCo lit the blunt on the table and sent it my way. After she handed me the blunt, she went behind Silk, pulled up her denim skirt, and began eating her from the back. After a few minutes passed, they switched positions and CoCo took her throne as the queen of the deep throat. I don't think Silk liked being outshined, so they decided to compete from one greedy mouth to the next. My knees buckled, causing me to stumble backwards, so they led me to the couch. Coco picked up where she left off with a mouth full of me while Silk inhaled a line of powder she had placed on her index finger. Once she had snorted her fair share, it was on.

Silk stood up over the couch, put her monkey in my face, and grabbed the back of my head, trying to force me to take a lick, but I was upfront with her.

"I don't know how to eat pussy."

"Well guess what, boo, Silk is going to teach you. Now stick your tongue out and let me feel it on my clit."

I did as I was told. She walked me through it, telling me when and how to move my tongue. Within minutes, she was coming in and around my mouth.

"Damn, can I get some of that?" Coco asked, lifting her head up from my lap. I nodded my head.

As I pleased Coco with my tongue, Silk slid the condom on me and went straight into cowgirl mode while screaming all kind of nasty shit at me.

"Damn, this dick big, boo. Do you like this wet-ass pussy? Is it tight enough for you?" She did something strange with her vaginal muscles, and everything tightened around my meat. "What about now, nigga? That pussy real tight; ain't it, daddy?"

I couldn't answer due to my mouth being occupied, but I managed to nod my head yes. It was my first piece of pussy, and it felt like nothing I had ever experienced before. There were all kinds of throbbing and vibrations causing me to react the same way. I filled the condom up with my swimmers in the first two minutes of her sitting on it. I knew what a two-minute man was and felt embarrassed as fuck, but she assured me that everything was okay.

"Don't worry about that, boo. Silk gon' help you fix that and put you right back in the game."

She popped something in her mouth then kissed me. I could feel something pill-size enter my mouth, and she told me to swallow it. The last thing I remembered about that night was my dick getting back hard.

Dog Food

When I woke up to Omar's knocks on the door, I was naked in bed with Sierra sleeping on top of my brick-hard unprotected dick.

Chapter Five:
No Laughing Matter

The day had finally come for me to hit the road to college. When I was done packing, we decided it would be cheaper for me to get a rental car and drive to my dorm than for my mama to ship my stuff. She worked an early shift, so we said our goodbyes earlier that morning. Omar stayed at the house to help me pack up the car.

"So this is it! Don't take your weak ass to Alabama and forget about us little people back here in Memphis," Omar said, shaking my hand and hugging me at the same time.

"I won't, but yo, send a nigga some of that big, Dog Food bread from time to time. This ain't the NFL; all I'm getting out of this is a free education."

"Is that all you want?" He looked around to make sure nobody was listening. "You sure you don't want me to send you Silk?"

"Hell yeah, send me her, too!"

"I told you not to fall in love with that strip ho. That's the ho's job to make you fall in love with the pussy."

41

"I didn't fall in love with her pussy, but her little sister, Sierra. That's a different story."

Omar looked confused. "Who's Sierra?"

"One of the bitches you had her bring with her. But guess what, nigga? One of them hos robbed me while I was sleep for the money y'all gave me. I woke up to a pocket full of lint and my ID." I started laughing.

"I didn't have her bring nobody. I had already paid the bitch for you to have a night with her. And why are you just now telling me that those bitches robbed you? Them hos about to give you yo' money back. I don't know a bitch from the club name Sierra; what's her stage name?"

We could hear police sirens nearby, but that was normal for Westwood, so we didn't think anything of it.

"I don't know her stage name, but I don't remember seeing her at the club either."

"I paid Silk to come by herself, Dee. She brought those bitches along on some fuck shit!"

"Stop hating, Big O. Don't get mad at me because Silk decided to hook a player up. I got to hit all three of them all night long. Silk and Coco were freaks, but there was something about Sierra that drove me crazy."

He had this fucked up look on his face. "What does this bitch Sierra look like?"

"I don't know what she look like. I was fucked up and it was dark, but I remember what the pussy felt like. We ran out of condoms so I hit that shit raw, but—"

"What the fuck is wrong with you? You don't hit no bitch raw unless it's your wife. You decided to fuck her raw, or did the bitch ask you too?"

"Why?"

Omar was pissing me off with all the random ass questions he was asking. He had me thinking he was jealous that Silk treated me better than she had treated him.

"Nigga, just answer the fucking question!"

"We kinda both agreed. There weren't any more condoms, so I went to sleep. When I woke up she was drooling all over my piece telling me how she ain't got shit and how she wanted to feel the real me, so I went for it."

"You're the dumbest nigga I know. I bet the bitch rode you and when you said you was about to nut she didn't move, huh? Then she hit you with that I'm on birth control bullshit too, right?"

I thought about it for a minute, and he was right; that's exactly how it went down. I didn't want to answer, so I just gave him a confirming look.

He snatched his cell phone out of his pocket and yelled at someone on the other end to give him Silk's number. He repeated the number to the person on the other end of the phone then hung up and dialed it.

"What's up, O? What I do wrong?"

He didn't answer me, but he had disappointment written all over his aged face. He hung up the phone after hearing the disconnected number message play and dialed a different number.

The sirens were getting louder and so did Omar's yell. "Goldie, you sure that's that bitch's number, because the shit saying it's disconnected."

He stood there listening for about thirty seconds. "Two weeks, huh? Since the party...right, okay!"

"What O? Tell me something, nigga! You asked me all those questions like I know what's going on. Tell me something."

The police sirens had gotten louder. We could finally see them turning down our street.

"Look like we about to find out," he mumbled.

"Damn, look at all the police cars. Mr. Roberts must have went up side his wife's head again," I said laughing. "That nigga right there is crazy."

The police passed up the Roberts' address and headed straight for us.

"Omar, you don't have your gun or drugs on you, do you?"

"Naw nigga, I'm straight. I think this shit right here has something to do with you though. Goldie said the bitch quit the club after your partying and was talking all kinds of fuck shit about you."

Dog Food

"About me, why? Stop playing."

"I'm not playing and I'm not about to help you out this shit either. You let them hos set your dumb ass up. Trust no bitch, remember? You'll remember that shit next time!"

He threw his arms in the air before the police had even requested us to. I was lost and didn't know what the fuck was going on, so I headed toward them with my hands at my sides.

"Don't move and keep your hands where we can see them," a young, black female officer yelled and then unbuttoned the strap over her gun.

"Which one of you is Demarcus Elder?"

I didn't get a chance to respond, because Omar had already pointed at me. "That's that dumb-ass nigga right there."

"Are you Demarcus Elder?"

I nodded my head.

"We need you to come downtown with us to answer a couple of questions regarding your whereabouts on the night of August 26th."

"Man, don't say shit without a lawyer," Omar yelled.

"That was my birthday night. I didn't do anything!"

"I said don't say shit, Demarcus! Learn to fucking listen to somebody besides yo' fucking mama, bitch."

45

"I ain't no bitch! And I didn't do anything. Why are y'all messing with me?"

The officer took her hand off of her gun and got into my breathing space. "If you didn't do anything then you have nothing to worry about. We need to speak with you about a Sierra Mosley, that's all."

"About what? I don't know her like that to be answering any of y'all questions."

"We will discuss all of that when we get downtown. Looks like you're all packed up? Are you headed somewhere?"

"No, I want to discuss it now!"

She looked at Omar who was frozen in his stance then back at me. "You were named as a suspect in her sexual assault case."

"What the fuck?" Omar said it like he was the one being accused of it. The officer continued like he hadn't interrupted her.

"We are not here to arrest you. We just need you to come downtown with us to answer a few questions."

"I didn't assault her; she grabbed me."

Omar walked up on me like he was going to hit me. "Shut your fucking mouth before I shut it for you. You need a fucking lawyer. This shit ain't a game, young nigga. I'm about to call the big man and get a lawyer sent down there to meet you. Don't say shit without the lawyer, not another fucking word. Do you hear me?"

Dog Food

I nodded my head yes and allowed the officer to escort me to the back of her police car uncuffed. We sat in front of my house for another fifteen minutes or so as she talked to a dispatcher. The other two officers that came in their own squad cars looked through my rental car's windows and then started talking to Omar. I don't know what they were saying to him, but I heard him scream.

"Man, that's some bullshit!" Then, he pulled out his cell phone and started making more calls.

When we made it downtown to the police department, known to the streets as 201, they sat me in a room to wait for my lawyer to show up. After four hours of waiting, one never did. An officer informed me that my mother had arrived and was in the lobby waiting for me, but since I was now eighteen, she wasn't allowed to come to the interrogation room with me. I didn't know shit about the law, but I was tired of waiting with my thoughts. When the investigator stuck his head back in the room to say he still hadn't heard from my lawyer, I told him I was ready to talk.

"Good afternoon, Mr. Elder. Are you sure you're ready to talk, or did you still want to wait on your lawyer?" He asked like he already knew I didn't have one coming.

"I'm ready to talk."

I'd never had beef with cops, because I never had a reason to interact with them in a negative way. But after meeting this pig, I knew I'd hate police from here on out.

"There's talking going around that you like to force little girls into having sex by restraint." He took a puff of his cigarette then continued, "Or so we heard. Is that true?"

He sat down into the wooden chair across the table from me and just stared at me for ten minutes. I had decided I wasn't going to answer his question as soon as he had asked it. But if answering him meant getting the George Clooney-looking nigga out my face so I could go back home, I'd give it a try.

"Where did you hear that? Because I've only had sex with grown women. And restraint sounds like force. I didn't force anybody to do shit."

"Well, let me ask you this. Did you or did you not have sex with a Sierra Mosley on the night in question?"

"I don't know her last name, but yes I had sex with a woman named Sierra, not a little girl! And it wasn't by force. She came and pulled me into the room with her."

"Did you know that she was only fourteen when you used your weight to pin her down on the bed?"

His line of questioning didn't make sense to me. She wasn't no fourteen; she couldn't be, nor did I pin her down and force sex on her.

Dog Food

"If that's what the bitch was going around saying, she's lying!"

"Here," he said, handing me a piece of paper and a pen. "Why don't you write down everything that happened that night, and we will let the courts make the decision on who's lying."

It was nothing to me to write down what happened, because I didn't rape her. Her sister, Silk, kept screaming she couldn't take no more and that she was going to sleep. Coco was already out, and I was sitting on the couch with my dick still hard from the *X* pill. Sierra walked in, kissed me on the neck, and said it was her turn.

She immediately took me into her mouth, and we got down after that. We had a few issues with the condoms hurting her, and after trying to find one with more lubrication, we gave up and went to sleep. I don't know how long we had been sleep, but I remembered her waking me up with her mouth and us agreeing to do it raw. The only reason I shot off in her was because she said she was coming too and didn't want me to stop. So I gave her what she wanted. *Damn, I had given her exactly what she wanted!* That shit was a setup, because thinking back to when I left the room that morning, Silk and Coco were already gone, leaving me there with Sierra.

When I handed the investigator my statement, he read it then waved it in the air. In less than thirty seconds, two officers entered the room. One was holding hand cuffs and the other began reading me my Miranda rights. The investigator stood up.

"Thank you. That was the quickest rape confession I've ever taken."

My bitch-ass lawyer finally showed up while I was being formally booked. After that, I had my mug shot taken, was fingerprinted, had DNA samples taken from me, and was processed in the system for sexual assault on a minor. The shit had just gotten real!

Chapter Six:
The Welcoming

"Hello?"

That was my third time saying it in the last two minutes. My mama wasn't talking. She only answered her phone, so I could listen to her sob. "Stop crying, Mama, I told you I didn't do it! It didn't even go down the way she's saying it did. You acting like you don't know your son!"

"Her statement says you were drunk and high, Demarcus! The reports from the lab said you had marijuana and ecstasy in your blood, and you confessed to being drunk. I don't know you, because my child doesn't use drugs!"

"You do know me! And it was my first time ever getting high," I pleaded, "It was my first time doing anything." I'm sure she wouldn't want to hear my next words, but I wanted her to know she had raised me better than what she was hearing about me. "It was even my first time having sex."

She smacked her lips, "Boy!"

"It was! I don't want you crying and feeling like you did a bad job in raising me. She lying on me, Mama! She just trying to fuck up my life."

"Why would that girl choose you of all people to lie on, Demarcus? You don't have nothing. If I'm broke, so are you! Even with your football mess, all that does is pays for your housing and schooling. You can't even wash your ass good yet. Make me understand why out of everybody in this world she decided to choose you?"

I thought about telling her that I had lied about being rich, but the thought of my life being over due to a childish fib hurt too much to say.

"You're just like yo' sorry-ass daddy."

She tried to say it soft so I wouldn't hear it, but I did. She had never compared me to my father before and the fact that she did pissed me off!

"What the fuck you mean I'm just like my daddy, huh? You won't tell me shit about the nigga, so how can I agree with you? I thought you were scared if we talked about the devil he's gon' start talking about us?"

"It's if you think about the devil—"

"I don't give a damn what it is," I yelled, cutting her off.

"Boy, I know you going through some stuff, but you better fix your mouth quick! Don't you ever call yourself disrespecting me or—"

"Or what? You gon' cut me off like you did my daddy? You claim you don't know who he is, but in the same breath you tell me I'm just like him. Which one is it? You think I'm lying about this rape shit, and I think you're lying about a lot of shit! Which one of us is right?"

"You better lower your voice and show some respect! Boy, did you forget who you're talking to?"

"No, I know exactly who I'm talking to."

My chest felt like it was going to explode if I didn't finally tell my mama how I was feeling. All these years of biting my tongue and doing everything to please her, she didn't even have my back when I needed her. At the first sign of trouble, she was ready to cut me out her life. I bet that's exactly what she did with my daddy. I had to make sure she knew how I felt before she threw me away, too.

"I know who I'm talking to. I'm talking to the real reason I'm behind these bars! You did everything you could so I wouldn't be like my daddy. You even made sure not to tell me the nigga's name. Lie after lie. One minute you were running the streets and didn't know who you were pregnant by, then the next minute he up and left when he found out you were pregnant. Which one is it? I think Auntie Cat was right when she said you were doing more than praying on your knees. Did you hate my daddy that much that you refused to teach your only son to be a man? That's crazy! My entire life I've been called all kinds of bitches, pussies, and ho-ass mama's boys. You never did anything to toughen me up.

You even tried to stop me from playing football because there were too many men involved, but you know what?"

I waited for her to respond, but she didn't say anything.

"I said, do you know what?"

I had been talking so much that I hadn't realized when or how long ago she had hung up. I slammed the phone on the receiver and started making my way down the hallway; then everything went black. Whatever had been thrown over my head was being held close to my neck, causing me to lose oxygen. My body was knocked down to the floor and I was covered in kicks and stomps. I couldn't even snatch whatever it was off my face because the kicks were landing there too.

"So, you like beating up little girls and taking the pussy?"

The voice was coming from someone doing the kicking on my right-hand side, because I could hear the heavy breathing between his words.

"Yeah he do. He's a bitch," another voice whispered, this time on the left of me.

I couldn't talk to verbally defend myself, and there were too many of them for me to try to defend myself physically. The beatings, accusations and insults kept coming until the computer in my head crashed and shut down. I woke up two weeks later in the county's hospital jail ward, recovering from multiple grand mal seizures followed by a medically induced coma.

A few days after I woke up, I'd stopped seizing and was showing signs of being able to use my motor skills. That's all those bitches were waiting on so they could send me to the infirmary in the jail. I was told I'd be in the infirmary for three weeks while my broken ribs and nose healed. Then, they'd send me right back into general population, so the ass whippings could continue.

One of the nurses at the county hospital said I had a couple of visitors while I was in a coma, and I was sure one of them had been my mama. Since the telephone calls in the infirmary were free, I gave her a call.

"Hello?" Omar answered the phone

"Put my mama on the phone."

"What up, nigga? You know she's at the hospital, but I heard about what happened to you. You straight?"

I didn't respond, not wanting to say the obvious.

"Man, I don't know why you ain't fucking with me all of a sudden. I keep telling you I didn't have shit to do with it, and if yo' ass would've listened..."

"Tell my mama I called."

"Wait!"

Omar knew I was ending the call, so he quickly said what he needed to say. "L.K. told me to tell you to use the lawyer he got you and to quit fucking with that public defender you came to court with. Dude ain't gone fight for you like the lawyer will. He keeps pushing back your court dates like you're guilty or something while the lawyer is setting up shit to get you a speedy trial and your charges changed from sexual assault to statutory rape with some other shit involved. You need to get with your lawyer, nigga." He kept going on and on, but the only thing that grabbed my attention was the lie I had caught the nigga in.

"L.K.? I thought you said you got me the lawyer? You even tried to tax my mama over the nigga!"

"I didn't try to tax yo' mama. She offered to help pay for him, and it doesn't fucking matter who got you the lawyer. You just make sure you use him, ho ass, young nigg—"

I hung up. Omar didn't know it, but that was the last time I was going to allow him, or anybody for that matter, to call me anything other than my name. Respect went both ways like confused sexuality, and niggas were sleeping on me if they thought that I was comfortable with the confusion. I knew it was my fault for giving Omar stacks of passes when I should've been giving him a corrective action plan, but we all learn from our mistakes. I used to be scared of the bitch nigga, but after being in this bitch for four months, all fear had gone AWOL.

Dog Food

Omar was right; it didn't matter who got the lawyer for me. But I'd be lying if I didn't say it made me feel a lot better knowing that lawyer's fees weren't on his or my mama's dollars. I didn't want my mama scraping up dimes to pay for the lawyer or for her to be in debt to Omar for getting me one. That's why I had fired him before we even sat down to talk. But on Lord King's dollar, hell yeah, I'd use him.

I was able to stretch my stay in the infirmary for another six weeks due to having random small seizures, and then they forced me back into population. The young Hispanic correctional officer I had gotten cool with from the infirmary escorted me to my cell and I thought round two of my jailhouse beating was about to begin. He put me in a cell with an older cat named Rico. Black and Deadly should've been his name. He had these beady eyes that made it seem like the nigga was constantly sizing you up through squints. His arms were an inch or two short of being the same size and length of his legs, making him short and stocky. Looking at him made you question if humans had really evolved from apes, because he mirrored the ones at the Memphis zoo with his shoulders hunched over and all.

"Mane, did you rape that young girl like these folks saying you did?"

His southern accent was deeper than our Memphis tongue. He had to be from Southern

Mississippi or the Boot. I threw my bags onto the top bunk and he snatched my shit right back off and held them in his oversized hands. I wasn't healed enough to take a beating from him, so I told him everything that had transpired that night. When I was done, he didn't say shit to me, he just threw my shit back on the top bunk then kissed some pictures of three young girls he had hanging on the wall. That was his way of letting me know he didn't play when it came to young girls. I vowed to learn how to sleep with one eye open.

The lawyer met with me about a week and a half before my court date and gave me my discovery package so I could know what was being said by the victim, arresting officers, the investigators and the toxicology lab. From the first page I read, the shit was filled with lies. The bitch Sierra said I had smothered her with a pillow, pinned her down using my elbows and then forced her to have sex. She said the more she cried, the more pain I caused her by ramming my fingers up her rectum. Then for the cherry topper on this shit pie, the arresting officers said they caught me trying to flee the state in attempt to run from the crime.

"That's some bullshit!"

I threw my package on the ground, forgetting Rico was sitting below me. He stood up and stared at me like he was going to kill me. I've never felt my heart beat so fast. I closed my eyes and braced myself for the impact of his first hit, but it never came. When I leaned over my bunk to see why the change of heart, he was reaching down to grab the package off the ground. He climbed back in the bunk, now out of eyesight, and I could hear him flipping through the pages. When they called us out our room for recreation, he took my papers with him.

"God is always there for those who live by His words," my mama would say to me every time I came to her in tears. For the first time in six months, I finally got to see it.

"Get off that bunk. You getting out this cell today!"

"Naw, I'm straight. Too many niggas out there want to fight me over my charges. The only reason they ain't running up in this cell on me is because of you."

Rico acted as if I hadn't said shit and started heading back through the cell's door. When he stepped in the hall he stopped with his back still facing me.

"I'm not gon' tell you again," he said.

I hadn't been to rec in months. Every time I tried to, there was always a nigga wanting to fight me over my shit like he was related to the lying bitch. I had been in so many fights in the past six months, you'd think I was a welterweight boxer. I wasn't scared to fight. I just wasn't raised to, but jail was changing me. In a way, it was raising me. When I walked in the day room, my suspicions had been confirmed.

"Come over here, Dee, before it goes off!" Rico was sitting at a table with three other older black guys who looked as rough as him. They were all staring up at the TV.

"The rape case of the high school football star and the almost greatest running back the University of Alabama coaches would have had the pleasure of receiving goes to trial tomorrow. Demarcus Elder, seen here in his final game as a senior..."

I turned away at the sight of myself on the screen and drowned out the reporter's words by listening to the conversation being held at the table.

"Aww, shut up, bitch! That ho is lying on him. Come have a seat with us, youngster."

Those words had come from Dro. I knew of him from watching his case on the news before they played the episode on *First 48*. He had been snitched on by his baby mama after killing three dudes over some gang shit. They didn't have shit on him until she told. The bitch was so trifling with the shit. She helped the police catch him by setting him up to meet her and their son at the local park for family time while he was on the run. He was only in my unit because he was waiting to get sent to the pen.

Dog Food

I sat down and instantly the whole table started helping me with my case. They started highlighting and circling key points that I needed to make sure my lawyer hit. This went on throughout my trial. Every time I returned from court, the niggas asked me to tell them what was said verbatim. All the work they had put in with my lawyer got my charges dropped to statutory rape which was only a class E felony. I was offered my freedom, using the eight months as time served with seven years of supervised probation. It was my first time getting into any trouble; that's why the book didn't get thrown at me. The second option given was to flatten my time, serve two years, and get out as a free man with no probation. I took option two, because I really didn't have anywhere to go. My mama didn't show up to any of my trial dates. When I called, she was always too sick, tired, or busy working to come visit. In our last conversation, she said somebody had come by the house saying they could get Sierra to say she was lying about it all for half a million dollars.

"Why would anybody think we had that kind of money just sitting around in a bank gaining interest?"

I knew why, but didn't say shit. Every call after that went to voicemail, and when Omar answered, he told me my mama was in and out the hospital like she lived there for days at a time.

With confirmation of Omar's snake-in-the-grass ass still living there, I knew I wasn't coming back to the same bullshit I'd left.

Jail had turned me into a man from all the fucked up stories I heard, the bullshit I had to see and the new life I had struggled to survive. I went from losing fights to walking away victorious. Everything was as good as it could get living behind bars, and then I was released.

Chapter Seven:
The Big "C"

It might sound crazy, but after being in jail for twenty-two months, five days, eight hours, thirty-seven minutes and however many seconds, everything about the world had changed to me. The streets didn't look or feel the same. The shit felt harsh, making me feel like I didn't belong. I was like a stray dog without a bone and no place to call home. I started missing the luxuries of jail. At least the bitch kept a roof over my head with three hot meals and a daily shower. I could still have all that if I took my ass back home to my mama, but that wasn't the decision I'd made. Fuck that. I wasn't going home to be treated like a baby or to beg for my mama's forgiveness. I wasn't the Demarcus she knew, and I wasn't about to readjust to fit back in. The city had turned cold, but I was frozen, so I'd survive.

Within my first two days of freedom, I almost fucked around and went right back to jail. I went to the police station by my mama's house to register as a sex offender and the little police bitch jumped crazy on me. The ho tried to say I was falsifying information because the address I gave her was for a vacant home they had just removed some trespassers from the night before.

"You must be thinking of another Bluebell Cove, because that's my mama's house."

The officer typed something faster than the way roaches moved when the lights came on into her computer then turned the screen around so I could see it.

"Is this your mama's house?" She had a smirk on her ugly, boxed-shape face.

There it was, clear as day, with a for sale sign in the yard. The doors had been snatched off and all the windows in front of the house had been shot out.

"What happened to the people who lived in it?"

"Who knows what happened to them? The sign on the outside of the door says police station not information booth! I need an address sex offender, one you actually live in."

"Bitch!" I couldn't stop it from coming out my mouth, so I tried to hurry and clean it up. "I mean officer, before I was locked up, I used to stay there with my mama. Is there a way for me to find out where she's at?"

She didn't respond to my question. She just wore a *fuck you* look on her face. "I need the address to where you're living at now before it's back downtown to lock up!"

Dog Food

I gave her evil ass the address to the motel I had checked into and told her I'd be there until I got a job and my own place. She gave me a stack of papers and told me I needed to update my address every time I moved. She reminded me that I couldn't live within a thousand feet of schools, childcare facilities, or the victim, then she smiled.

"We'll make sure to let the neighborhood know you're here, and I hope everybody welcomes you back home!"

I wanted to talk funky to the bitch, but I let it go. Going by my mama's house became my first priority. Maybe I could find something or someone around there that would know where she had moved.

When I made it to the house, it looked exactly like the picture but ten times dirtier. Old beer bottles covered the porch and there was trash from a turned over trash can all over the yard. It didn't feel right to let the shit just sit there, so I started cleaning it up.

"That ain't gone help, son. Those junkies will be right back tonight fucking it right back up," Mr. Roberts, the neighbor from two houses down said, joining in with the cleanup.

"Where did my mama move to? I thought she owned this house."

"She did, well almost. She had taken out some loans to fix it up over the years. When she fell sick, she couldn't afford to keep up with them."

"Fell sick?"

He looked at me with confusion written all over his wrinkled face.

"Yeah, you didn't know?"

"Didn't know what?"

He put the trash he had collected in the bin and sat it upright. "I'll let your uncle tell you. He'll be here getting high with everybody else later on tonight. That fool spent all that time in jail dodging dick to come out to a glass one."

I didn't give a fuck about Uncle Leroy or his new venture. I wanted to know about my mama! "Mr. Roberts, with all due respect, what the fuck happened to my mama?"

He sat there staring at the trash for a second or two then said, "She got the 'Big C' a few months back. Last I heard, she was living in Baptist hospital."

"The Big C? You mean my mama got cancer?"

He nodded his head up and down.

"Can I get a ride up to Baptist, Mr. Roberts? All I have is the six hundred dollars left that my mama had put on my books, and I'm living in a thirty dollar a night motel, but I can give you gas money."

He shook his head no. "I'll take you up there, son. I don't need any gas money."

Dog Food

I hopped out the car at the hospital and told Mr. Roberts not to wait, because I'd be staying up here with her. He shook my hand tightly and slid me two hundred dollars from the palm of his hand.

"This is all I got son, but come by and see me every now and then on Sundays. I'll make my wife cook us up a good meal. There's always yard work to be done if you're looking for work to pay for a night or two at the motel."

I thanked him for the money and accepted the job nonchalantly, because getting up to my mama's room was the only thing on my mind.

"We don't have a Sharon Elder here, honey," the older, gray-haired black nurse said, looking at me over her glasses instead of looking through them.

"Yes, y'all do! Can you look again? My neighbor said she was here getting treated for cancer."

She must have seen the desperation on my face, because she looked again and made multiple phone calls. "Baby, she isn't here. I've called every hospital in Memphis. No one has a Sharon Elder as a patient. I'm sorry to hear about your mama having cancer baby, but she isn't here."

I knocked everything I could off the front desk and kicked the base of the counter. "I know she's here! My mama has cancer. Where else in

Memphis could she be? You need to get off your old ass and go check some rooms!"

I watched the younger black nurse who had been sorting through charts snatch the phone off the wall and call security as the lady who was assisting me tried to calm me down.

"I don't know where she is baby, but you need to calm down. I'm not about to go checking rooms for no ghost! Go home. Maybe she was already released."

"Calm down for what? Y'all hiding my mama. Did she tell y'all not to let me know she was here?" I screamed at her, "Y'all bitches want to play games?"

The security officer grabbed me from the back of my arm and I slung his tall, skinny black ass to the floor.

"What room is my mama in? One of y'all bitches needs to tell me something now!"

I heard the nurses telling the security officer to gently escort me out and to call the police if I refused to leave, so I ran through the front doors before he grabbed me again and I caught a new case. I couldn't stop running. Honestly, it felt good to run for a minute. Then it hit me that running through the city at top speed would be the only running I'd ever do again. Thinking of how football wasn't in my future anymore over that lying ass bitch filled me with anger. When I finally got my thoughts together, I was standing at the information desk at Methodist hospital where my mama worked, and I was out of breath.

"Is Sharon Elder at work today? I'm her son, Demarcus Elder."

"Demarcus Elder? The college running back who raped that girl at the motel?"

The nigga started sizing me up like if my answer was yes, he was going to put his hands on me. He didn't know it, but his fat ass didn't want any of these problems I had to offer. I had whooped niggas twice his size in jail, but I didn't mind adding his sloppy yellow ass to the list.

"Yeah, that Demarcus Elder, my nigga."

He took his walkie-talkie out the holder on his hip and sat it on his desk. "Let me holla at you outside for a minute."

"Aww, you need to holla at me?" I laughed. "Are you sure you want to do that?"

"Nigga, that's my little cousin. I need that one, but I ain't about to stop feeding my family over it! Otherwise I'd knock you off yo' ass right here, ho."

I let the nigga lead the way out the hospital, but I noticed he was heading toward the employee parking lot. He was stupid if he thought I was going to let him make it to his car to get his heat. I snuck the nigga from the back then worked his fat ass out like I was his personal trainer. I left the nigga leaking, face down in a mixture of wet grass and damp gravel and then dipped without finding out if my mama was there. It took me three hours to get back to my mama's house on the bus, and just like Mr. Roberts had said, the porch was covered with junkies with my uncle acting as the ring leader.

"Uncle Leroy!"

He was sky high, singing and doing the mashed potato on the porch with a smoked out prostituting bitch by his side.

"*I can mash potato, doop, doop, doop. I can do the twist, doop, doop, doop. Now tell me baby, doop, doop, doop. Who pimping like this*?" he sang.

"Get it, baby," the ho cheered on, dancing on the side of her man like only a faithful ho would.

He had on what was supposed to be a mustard yellow suit, but it was caked with filth. His shirt and gold chains were missing, but his nappy chest hairs were still there and so was his hat. He looked like a fucked up rendition of Al Green performing *Tired of Being Alone* on Soul Train.

"Uncle Leroy!"

He stopped dancing and took a sip of his beer. "That voice right there sounds familiar. It's a lot deeper than I remember it being, and the bitch ain't in it. Nephew!"

I cracked the nigga so hard that he hit the floor and his bottle shattered on the ground. I cocked my fist back and stood over him just in case he needed another one to help him watch his mouth.

"Where the fuck is my mama?"

"What the fuck is wrong with you, Dee? I ain't seen you in years and the first thing you do to your favorite uncle is pop me in my damn mouth?"

"You ain't my favorite uncle, nigga. If I have to ask you where my mama is again, me popping you in the mouth will be your last worry."

He started staggering, trying to get his self back up, but was too high to regain his footing. "Well damn, can you at least help me up, nephew?"

I grabbed the nigga by his arm, stood him up, and then leaned him against the house for balance.

"Little nigga, you done got strong. Look at you, looking like Omar! Boy, give me a hug."

He tried to take a step closer, and I squared up on him. When he saw I meant business, he leaned back against the house.

"Where's my mama, Unc? Mr. Roberts said she was at Baptist Hospital, but they said she ain't there. Where in the fuck is she?"

He straightened out his clothes like he used to do back in his pimping days. "Naw Demarcus, she ain't at Baptist no more. She's at Memorial Park."

He then mumbled under his breath, "This nigga just fucked up my suit."

"Where's Memorial Park Hospital at? How do I get there from here?"

He looked at me for a minute, and then placed his hands on my shoulders. "Memorial Park ain't a hospital nephew; it's a cemetery. Your mama passed right before summer. She's been dead going on three months now. Let your uncle hold a dollar or something coming around here asking me about hos that ain't on my payroll. You fucked up my high and scared my ol' lady."

I threw two punches and the whole porch took off running. One knocked my uncle out and the other landed through the already broken window. I had shards of glass going up my arm like women's bracelets. I couldn't feel the pain in my arm, just the one deep down in my chest. I fell on top of my uncle's sleeping body and cried, asking him why until I fell asleep. I woke up to the police harassing us for trespassing.

We were taken down to the police station, and Unc talked shit the entire ride there. "Do you know who the fuck I am? I'm the James Brown of this pimping shit. I'm like Elvis to his fans to my hos, I'll never die. I'm legendary, check the pimp chronicles. They got a whole chapter dedicated to me. Now let me go before I sue y'all asses for reckless endangerment of a pimp. Real niggas are a dying breed. Tell 'em, Dee! They broke the mold when they made me!"

I wasn't about to tell them shit. When we made it to the station, they let me go with a warning. Unc was arrested as a repeat offender, but I didn't give a fuck about him. I just wanted to get back to my room and cry the shit out.

A part of me wanted to go to her grave, but I wasn't ready for that visit yet. There was nothing I could do or say to her six feet deep that would change the fact she died thinking I hated her. Now I could honestly say I understood how my mama felt over her last interaction with Auntie Cat. But I refused to let what I said change me like her words to her sister changed her. It would've been nice if our last conversation was full of smiles and love, but that was fairytale thinking. Life wasn't structured that way, and to keep it real, I had already decided I wasn't fucking with my mama the day I got released. I spent my last six months in jail shielding my heart from her. I wanted her out of my life and cancer had given me exactly what I wanted.

Chapter Eight:
Help Wanted

"I'm sorry, Mr. Elder. We can't hire you with this type of felony. The majority of our employees are women. I wouldn't want them to be uncomfortable because you are around. Anyways, I wish you the best of luck in your job search."

Five interviews, five rejections, and only five days' worth of money to pay for my motel room and food. I didn't know what the fuck I was supposed to do. I was up and out the door by seven every morning, putting in ten applications per day, seven days a week, for the last three weeks, and I had only been called back for five interviews. Something was wrong with those numbers, and it was my felony. What made this shit even worse was when I had days like this, there was no one for me to talk to about it. I didn't have any friends; I lost them when I caught my case. I didn't have any family; they had orphaned me before I decided to orphan off myself. There were no women in my life, because I learned the hard way not to trust a bitch. I wasn't like them niggas in jail who were counting down their days to go home and get into some pussy. I'd beat my dick 'til it was bruised before I trusted another bitch with it. With no one in the streets to converse with, I wrote my nigga Rico a letter.

Rico,

I'm out here with all these fake ass-niggas, so I thought I'd hit a real nigga up. What's good with you big bruh? I know you're keeping your head to the sky, so I ain't worried about you.

Man, the city is different now. Seems like everybody out here has turned cold-hearted. I touched down to find out my mama died of cancer while I was locked up and my bitch-ass cousin who lived with her didn't even write or visit to tell me. I can't wait to run into the nigga!

I'm staying at a motel off of Bill Morris Parkway at the Ridgeway Road exit, but I don't know for how much longer because I can't get a job for shit! Ain't nobody rushing to hire sex offenders, and the jobs I know I can do, I can't apply for because I got to keep my distance from kids. Shit's fucked up out here, but you'll see it for yourself soon.

I'll see you in six months if you don't go home to Mississippi, and hopefully I'm straight by then so we can have a drink. You know I'll be twenty-one next month. Niggas ain't gon' be able to tell me nothing! Hit me up on the address on this envelope. It's my old neighbor's house. They'll make sure I get it.

> *Stay up,*
> *Dee*

I dropped Rico's letter in the mail on my way to Mr. Roberts' house to work. He had me raking leaves, and then I helped him change the oil in both of their vehicles. He paid me one hundred and twenty dollars and gave me a pair of clean clothes that belonged to his son, Adam, who was in the military. The black V-neck sweater Mr. Roberts had given me was a little too small, but it complemented my torso. Adam and I must have been the same height and size from the waist down, because the stone washed jeans fit perfectly. I wasn't comfortable with wearing another nigga's shit, but I didn't have any clothes other than what I had been arrested in, and that shit was too short and tight. I laced up his hush puppies which were a half of size too big and made the most of it. Mr. Roberts said Adam was on his second term and was never home to wear any of it. He told me to take as many of his clothes as I could fit and claim them as my own. I did as I was told. I had to give Adam his props, because he had an original swag about his style. It was business casual with a touch of hip hop. All of his clothes in the closet were hung by outfit. His shoes were next to the matching outfit, still in the shoe boxes. I could tell he was a little bit older than me, because even the lounging clothes he had in his drawers were on the dressier side of relaxing. I took advantage of the opportunity to get cleaned up and utilized the clippers he had on his bathroom sink to line myself up. My face was covered in hair which I hadn't had before going to jail. I didn't know how to clean it up, but I knew the look I wanted. I left a patch of hair on my chin, trimmed it down some to kill that goat look, and shaved everything else off. I checked myself out from head to toe in the hallway mirror before heading downstairs for dinner, and there he was. Omar was standing face to face with me through my reflection. We were identical now except for his battle wounds. That's if he hadn't been through any major physical changes in the past three years. Having my nose broken and all of those stressful, sleepless days and nights had finally corrected the only two major differences between us. I looked deep in my reflection's eyes like I was staring into Omar's. "You're dead on sight, ho!"

I could've stood there mugging myself and talking shit for hours, but I put my hate for Omar on hold to enjoy the meal Mrs. Roberts had cooked up. It was at her husband's demand, which could've been a physical one, because his ex-marine ass didn't play when it came to calling the shots or punishing insubordination. Before getting to know him, the only thing I knew about him was that he was the crazy nigga from down the street that kept getting arrested for hitting his wife. Mr. Roberts was cool though, and although the police came frequently to his house on some domestic shit, I knew that nigga really loved his wife. He was seated on the left of her at the four-person roundtable kissing her all over her wrinkled face when I made it downstairs. He had cleaned himself up also and was wearing the same colors as me.

To the left of him was an unknown guest that looked like a thick slice of heaven on earth to me. I had never seen a woman more beautiful than the one I was filling my hungry eyes with. She had this warmth about her with a brownish-gold skin tone to match. She wasn't naked; her complexion was only visible by her face and hands. From the neck down she was fully dressed, wearing a cocaine-white turtle neck with khaki-colored slacks. Her hour glass shape seeped through her clothes, giving her a sexy, business-professional look, but something about her eyes said she was hood. That might be the reason she was wearing non-prescription glasses, to try and hide her true side. Her eyes were round and slanted toward the ends like commas. For a second, I got lost in their darkness. Looking into her eyes, I could tell that baby girl had seen some shit, yet the stories of her past lied in her looks. Her round, pie-shaped face with those full, come-kiss-me lips and barely visible dimples made my dick jump.

It wasn't the animal reaction that surprised me, it was the feeling she made me feel in my heart that did. I don't know why, but the sight of her made me want to love every part of her, inside and out, and help her deal with whatever it was that lie beneath. She made me want to go out and hustle hard to spoil her, and I didn't know shit about her. I was on some slow, romantic R&B shit in my head before I had even gotten her name. The longer I looked at her, the more I wanted to wrap her long pony tail around my hand and pull on it until it made her head tilt back so I could lay soft kisses up and down her long neck that I bet was perfumed. The room caught me staring at her, but she handled it with confidence.

"You must be Demarcus," she said while getting up from her chair to shake my hand. "I'm glad to finally get to meet you, and even happier that you made it downstairs so we can finally eat." She smiled at me and then at the Roberts. "By the way, my name is Bria."

I shook her hand and thought hers would melt from the heat she had me giving off. I didn't mean to, but I had held her hand a second too long, and she gently moved it away from my grip.

The softness of her skin left me wanting to feel it again, but not from her hand. I wanted to find out just how much of her body was as soft. I almost didn't eat from watching her move the fork in and out of her mouth. The shit was erotic. If it wasn't for my pants, my meat would've broken through the table. I turned my focus to my plate and immediately the food blocked out my thoughts of Bria. I had to give it to Mrs. Roberts, the food was on point. I felt bad about thinking it, but my mama didn't have shit on Mrs. Roberts in the kitchen. We laughed and joked over our meal, which was different from the silent meals I grew up having. Bria was the life of the party. She made sure silence never found a seat at the table. She didn't talk about anything of importance, but she kept the conversation flowing. The atmosphere made me feel like I was a part of the family and not a paid yard worker.

Mrs. Roberts started clearing off the table with her husband's help. I took their absence as an opportunity to try to get to know Bria a little better. "Bria, what do you do for a living, beautiful?"

She took her glasses off like they were a part of a costume she had been wearing that hid the world from knowing who she really was.

"Look Demarcus, you can save all that beautiful shit for the birds. I don't need you to compliment me on my looks or intelligence, because I already know my worth. And stop staring at me with your mouth wide open like you've never seen a woman before." She took her hair out of the pony tail holder and shook her head until her hair relaxed on her shoulders before continuing. "That little staring move you tried to pull when you brought yo' ass downstairs wasn't original, nor is this weak-ass conversation you thought you could spark up when my aunt and uncle walked out the room. You can save it! I'm here to help you get a roof over your head then bounce. What in the hell would I want with a broke nigga who already needs me more than I need him? Let's keep this shit professional; you're not on my level to make this shit personal!"

I was lost for words. I wanted to say something that would cut her like her words had cut me, but I didn't know what the fuck she was talking about! She said she was here to help me get a roof over head. How, and when? I gave her the win over my game being weak, but it was the first in my life that I tried to spit some. She could have given me a pass for not perpetrating a fraud, but she was too stuck up to respect my feelings. I decided to give her a piece of what she had dished out, because I could tell she wasn't used to getting any of it back.

"Calm down before you let your mouth kill your looks, sweetheart! I didn't know you were invited over here to try and help me out, or I would've made sure I didn't show up today. I'm

Dog Food

not looking for charity. My shit is funky right now, but I'd sleep in the streets before I make kissing your snobby ass a priority. The better question is what did your uncle tell you about me that got you sitting here going hard on me and shaking your hair at me like I ain't shit?" I didn't give her time to answer. "I told you were beautiful before you opened up that nasty-ass mouth you got, and at that time, you were to me. But I take it back! And about you having intelligence, I don't recall ever saying that because you showing me right now you dumb as fuck if you thought a nigga was gon' hound you." I stood up and started making my way from the table. "I'm gone! Tell your aunt and uncle I said thanks for everything, and by the way, you ain't all that perfect like you think you are. You got greens stuck in your off-white ass teeth, sweetheart!"

I left her sitting there silent. Baby was bad, but not bad enough to let her belittle me so she could feel better about herself. She didn't know my background with women, and with how funky her attitude was, she wouldn't be the one to make it better in my future!

About three weeks later, I thought I heard a knock on my room's door, but I wasn't sure because I was working out with the clock's radio on. The knocks got harder. Standing there looking plain as hell in some oversized gray sweats, a white, extra tight t-shirt, scuffed up black-and-white running shoes, with no glasses on was Bria with bags in both hands.

"What's up?" I asked, dry as fuck, blocking her entrance into my room. If she wanted a do over she was going to have to humble herself and beg for one.

"I had stopped by to check on my aunt and my uncle asked if I could bring by these bags of clothes you left and your mail."

I snatched the bags out of her hands. "Thanks!" Then, I forcefully closed the door in her face.

I hit thirty more pushups to give her time to leave then peeped through the window to make sure she was gone, but she wasn't. She was at her car pulling her hair up in a ponytail. She popped the trunk, grabbed a large folder, and then started heading back to my door. I ran to the bathroom so she wouldn't know I was standing by the window watching her. I made her knock three times then snatched the door open like I was irritated.

"What now, Bria?"

"Dang, you don't have to say it like that, Demarcus! Can I show you some stuff? All I need is like ten minutes."

"I'm busy."

"Busy doing what in this raggedy-ass motel room?" she snapped.

Dog Food

"Doing me, in my raggedy-ass motel room! I got roaches and everything up in here. I don't want you scared. You know how beneath you I am." I chuckled trying to sound as corny as I possibly could.

"That's why I pulled my hair up and wore clothes I don't care about over here. I'm going to burn them and take a flea bath when I leave from here," she said, pushing me out of the way like she was running shit.

Bria was disgusted, and it was all over her face, but she surprised the hell out of me. She lifted the overflowing trash can and sealed the bag then headed out the door. She came back a few minutes later with an armful of clean bedding and cleaning supplies I could tell belonged to the hotel. She put on some plastic gloves and went to work. She started throwing away all the fast food cups I had started collecting to have as dishes when I moved into my own place. She didn't ask me what was trash or what I wanted to keep. She just took it upon herself to throw shit away. Bria hadn't said say a word since she started cleaning and, feeling like I wasn't helping, I joined in. When the room was spotless, she finally spoke.

"Are you ready to take a look at some stuff? I'm sorry, but my mind doesn't function around filth."

Bria didn't know it, but she had just submitted her application for being my woman with her bougie ass.

Chapter Nine:
A Peak at Sunshine

Bria had left me a stack of information on local men's shelters and printoffs of ads for live-in help in exchange for housing. She was an advocate for the homeless, and at only twenty-three years old, she was managing her own caseload. She knew what she was talking about when it came to getting people off the street, but as I read through the folder, I knew something that she apparently didn't know. She didn't know that I couldn't meet the criteria to apply, because the majority of them didn't welcome felons or sex offenders. The ones that did made me want to hustle harder to ensure I'd never have to live in them. Going through them had killed my mood, but then I opened Rico's letter.

Dee,
I'm sorry to hear about your mom passing, but happy you still have your freedom. That's fucked up your cousin didn't reach out to you, but your time would have been harder if you would have

known. I'm on my countdown to freedom and you know I'm taking my ass back to Biloxi, Mississippi. My kids need me and I've been gone too long. I know it's discouraging to keep being turned down for jobs, but know God has something special for you and what He has for you, no man can touch. My brother-in-law is a foreman at a warehouse right there over the Arkansas/Tennessee Bridge in West Memphis, Arkansas. I can't promise you the job, but you should go holler at him and drop my name. The name of the plant is Sheet Metal Crafting and his name is Paul. Hope everything works out for you, and if I ain't already too late, happy birthday nigga. Now stop being scared of women and get you some pussy!

Much love,
Rico

Rico had given me the best birthday gift ever, because when I walked in Sheet Metal Crafting on my birthday, I left with a thirteen-dollar-per-hour job as a laborer. I took my employment papers straight to Mr. Roberts to ask for a loan until my weekly payday, so I could keep a roof over my head. Instead, he and Mrs. Roberts paid my room up for two weeks as my birthday gift. The Roberts had become family, and once I figured out how to make their niece fall in love with me, we'd be related by marriage. I was learning Bria, and one of the lessons she

Dog Food

unknowingly taught me was that she didn't respect niceness. She'd walk right over it and would leave you feeling vulnerable. I had learned that much about her and wouldn't make the mistake twice. I had mentioned to her that it was my birthday this Monday. When she asked what I was doing, I changed the subject and she didn't like it.

"Why are you so secretive about your birthday plans? You must be about to get into something you don't have any business doing."

"Naw, I'm just chillin'."

"Chilling how, Demarcus?"

I shrugged my shoulders.

"I'm asking because if you don't have any major plans, I'd like to take you to get something to eat or something."

"I'll let you know what's up."

I waited until that Sunday and called her from her uncle's house to tell her that we could go out. A part of me wanted to, but the other part of me felt like I shouldn't be going if I couldn't pay for our meal. After going back and forth with her about my finances and what a man is supposed to do, we agreed on her cooking for me at her place.

Bria picked me up around six o'clock because I told her I had to get up early to catch a ride from Mr. Roberts to get to work. She was looking fresh out of the Grammys. She had on a tight, all-black, ankle-length, strapless dress and some red and black heels with a red purse to match. Her hair was down in big curls, and she smelled like a newly opened bottle of honey. I didn't look bad myself in an all-black button up with black slacks and black boat shoes to match, compliments of Adam. She was too dressed up to be just cooking at the house.

"Where are we going?"

"You'll see," she laughed.

We took the US-61 straight out and ended up in Tunica, Mississippi, at the casino. I didn't have to tell her that it was my first time, because she could see my reaction at finally being able to gamble that it was.

"Wait, before we go in I got you something." She went to her trunk and took out an envelope and a huge bag full of stuff. "This is for your birthday," she said, handing me the card. "And this is for your new job."

I opened up the card and there were five crisp hundred dollar bills in it. Before I could protest she said,

"You gotta have money to gamble and to take me out to eat."

Then I opened the bag. There were some steel-toe boots in it, a hard hat, a safety vest, and some work gloves.

"I thought you'd need them, working in a warehouse and all."

Dog Food

I leaned down and kissed her on the cheek, and then grabbed her by the hand and took off to the casino's doors.

"Come on, we got money to win."

The casino wasn't ready for us. I hit for eighteen hundred dollars in my first fifteen minutes on the slots and was ready to bounce. I handed Bria eight hundred, and she refused to take it.

"No, that's your birthday gift! I don't want it back."

"You gave me five. I'm giving you eight. I'm just splitting my winnings with you."

"I don't want any of the money you won. In your situation, you need the money way more than I do."

"I was wondering when you were going to show your true colors. In my situation, huh? You mean me being broke and homeless? I've been looking at you as a friend, but now I know what it is. I'm another homeless ass nigga on your caseload."

She snapped back. "I didn't mean it like that, Demarcus!"

"So how did you mean it, Princess Bria?"

She didn't answer, because she couldn't. Her silence let me know that my birthday outing was just her doing her advocacy work.

"Here!" I dropped the money on her lap. "That's for the work stuff you got me and the five you gave me. Keep the change, so you can buy yourself something to eat. This ain't a date. I'm not paying for your shit. Remember, I'm broke!"

The hurt she wore looked good on her face. I walked away from the slots and left her sitting there to think about what she had done. She found me feeding my face at the casino's buffet.

"I'm sorry, Demarcus. I swear I didn't mean it that way. Yes, you're in a messed up situation with your mama dying and leaving you homeless, but I'm not your advocate nor am I your caseworker. I'm here with you, celebrating your birthday as your friend."

"I bet."

"I am! How can I look down on you when I once was in your shoes?"

"I doubt you were in my shoes, not the way you act."

"How do I act?"

"Like an uppity-ass, spoiled bitch that ain't been through any real shit to humble your ass."

She sat in the seat next to mine and moved closer to me until our legs touched. "You need to watch that bitch word. You damned right I'm spoiled by me! What you don't know is that I've earned the right to act like this. I crawled before I walked. Now I'm sprinting, and you will do the same. I work in this field as a constant reminder of where I've been and how, if I fall off, I could be right back there! My past did humble me, but I'm

Dog Food

not the weak victim to life as I once was, and I'm not going to walk around like I am."

I knew her eyes held a story that she needed to get out, but here wasn't the place. Before she spilled her guts in the overcrowded buffet, I placed my index finger over her mouth. "Let's go somewhere else and talk."

We rode back to my room listening to the sounds of the road. Not a word was spoken. I knew when she was ready to get the monkey off her back she would. I didn't want to pressure her into anything.

Everything about Bria was unpredictable except her attitude. She walked in my room, kicked off her heels, and sat Indian style on my bed with a pillow propped behind her back and another on her lap.

"Hand me those pizza delivery papers off the table. Everybody didn't get to eat at the buffet like you."

I handed them to her and asked her to order one for me as well.

"Sure, what kind do you want? And I hope you know you're paying for it. This ain't no date!" She smiled at me with her last words, and I felt myself melting away. The sadness had left from her face, and I was happy to see it gone.

"You need to fix your mouth, baby girl. As a matter of fact come here, so I can fix it for you!"

She didn't move. "If you want to fix my mouth, you'll need to come to me!"

"Is that right, smart ass? Then I guess it will just have to stay funky, but you know that means don't you?"

"What does it mean?" She had a flirtatious smile on her face.

"We can't be friends no more. I don't have friendships with people that have funky mouths." I folded my arms and turned my back to her like a small child ending a friendship.

She started dying laughing, but her laugh was getting closer to me until it tickled the hairs on the back of my neck. She turned me around, unfolded my arms, and softly kissed me on the lips. "Then I guess we can't be friends. And, since we ain't dating like you've announced all night, I guess you'll just have to settle for being my man."

We kissed and grabbed, letting our hands roam all over each other's bodies. She tried to snatch my shirt open like some shit seen on a movie, but only one button broke. We fell out laughing, instantly killing the mood. I lifted my shirt over my head, but left my muscle shirt on, and took her hand in mine. I led her to the wooden chair at the table and sat in it. I lifted her dress up, revealing a black thong, and made her straddle my lap. Common sense had kicked in for the first time, and before we went any further, we needed to talk.

Dog Food

"Look at me, beautiful." I cupped her chin in my hand and gently turned her face until we were eye to eye. "Do you know what you're saying and who you're saying it to? Look around you; this is all a nigga got."

"I know what you got. You got everything in this room."

She reached in with her lips to kiss me, but I turned my head so it landed on my cheek. She was talking with her pussy. I could feel the heat and dampness through my slacks. But I needed to talk to her heart and mind. If what she was saying to me was real, I'd have time to talk to her second set of lips later.

"I'm serious Bria. I don't have a car to come see you in or a cell phone to call you on. I don't have any of the things I need to keep a relationship afloat. But, if you believe in me like the shit you said about me crawling and sprinting and are willing to give me time, I'll have all that. In time, I'll be able to give you everything that you need, but you can't break bad on me during the struggle."

She started getting off of my lap. "Demarcus, you're talking too serious for me. I know what you're saying, but it sounds like moving in together, marriage, and kids to me. I'm not ready for none of that right now. I just want to take things slow and get to know each other better."

"I hear what you're saying, but to me it sounds like you saying you can't be faithful." I joined her in standing up. As she looked up into my eyes, I looked down into hers.

"I can be faithful, but I've been hurt before, badly. I'm feeling you, everything about you. I'm feeling your hazel eyes, your wide, toned body, and those firm ass lips."

Everything she said was physical. Where was the other shit like me being smart, caring, or a go-getter? Out of nowhere Omar's words, *trust no bitch,* ran across my thoughts. "How old are you? Let me see your driver's license!"

"What are you talking about now, Demarcus? What do you need to see my license for?" She asked the questions laughing, but still reached into her strapless bra to show it to me.

I didn't bother looking at it, because I knew I was tripping. She was of age and she knew I was broke, but I needed her to say something deeper than the flesh. "If all I wanted was a nut, Bria, there's this little, thick-ass bitch upstairs selling pussy. She already said she'd give me a discount for living here."

She thumped me in my mouth. "Stop playing with me Demarcus. If all I wanted to do was get fucked, I'd find me a nigga with some money to pay for my services. Don't laugh at what I'm about to say to you and don't think I'm crazy. But I've wanted you since you checked me at my aunt and uncle's house. I knew I had to have you when you slammed the door in my face. I've never had a man keep it that real with me, and that's exactly what I've been looking for."

She laughed and grabbed both of my hands and stood on her tippy toes until her lips felt like a whisper on my mine. "I knew you were the man that would be able to tame me and teach me how to trust again. All I ask of you is not to break my heart."

I took her dress off and scooped her up from the ground like ice cream. I cut my mind off and let my soul control my movements. I kissed every dry spot on her body and tongue-kissed every place that contained moisture. After twenty minutes or so of listening to her beg through moans, I gave her what she'd been asking for. I dipped in and pulled right back out to release. I wasn't prepared for what she had to offer and it was my first nut as a free man, but I didn't need a pill this time to get back up. As fast as my release came, I was ready for my second trip to her uncharted waters.

Her grip, combined with the warm wetness, sent chills up my spine with each stroke. I shook with every pump as if I was in a freezer, but she was on fire. Bria moved her body like a gymnast with the way she rested her knees on her shoulders to welcome all of me inside of her. I accepted the welcoming and slid in until her body made me stop and my balls prevented me from diving deeper. When I freed her breast from her bra to pacify my mouth, a condom fell to the bed. I grabbed it and showed it to her.

She shrugged her shoulders and said, "Wishful thinking?"

I applied the rubber, which I should have done from the start, and then no-handed my way back in. The sensation to nut had calmed down, and it was on. With a mouthful of both of her breasts, I gave it to her every way our bodies could turn with me on top. I flipped her over to her stomach and pushed her knees up until they were under her breast and beat her like a drum. She started screaming in pleasurable pain and didn't stop until the person occupying the next room banged on the wall. I slowed the beating down, but apparently it was too slow for her.

"Let me sit on it, Daddy. It's my turn to drive."

She moaned like something heard on a porno as I went in deep one last time before changing up. I got on my back and when she was secured in her new position of control, I licked and teased her nipples with my tongue. She took advantage of running the show and lifted my head off the bed, demanding that I suck on her breast. I didn't like the feeling of just lying there dead, so I began lifting my waist and stroking back. Her moans got deeper until they turned into words.

"Grab my ass."

Dog Food

I grabbed it, but not the way she wanted me to and she had no problem in correcting me.

"Grab it harder! Squeeze my cheeks together and put all of it in me."

Her words mixed with her juices now covering my lap and stomach were too much for me to handle. The battle ended with our explosions colliding. I was upset that I couldn't last longer, but in all actuality, it wasn't minutes that had passed, it was hours. Time had escaped us, and before I could check the time on the clock on the wall, Mr. Roberts was knocking at the door to take me to my first day of work.

Chapter Ten:
Hunger Pangs

Bria had me feeling like a new man. I stopped stressing over the day-to-day and got on my shit. I was working twelve hour days, five days a week, trying to stack up to get an apartment and car. She didn't complain about it, but I knew she was tired of dropping me off and picking me up from work every day. That's why I worked twelve hours and not the scheduled eight, to give her time to rest in between travels. Things were looking good for me, and then I got greedy...

The next two months, I had been keeping my eyes on this older cat I worked with named Greg, but some of the people we worked with called him Gutta. Gutta had been working at the plant for eight years and was the shift supervisor over my department. I heard niggas talking about how he was bringing in twenty dollars an hour or more for walking around not doing shit but making sure that we were busting our asses. They were saying how he started in the same position as us and how the warehouse had made him rich. They sat around dreaming about the day it would be their turn to move up. I laughed to myself and left the break room, because I was tired of listening to the idiots' huddle. It wasn't in me to get excited over what the next nigga had. That's why I didn't watch music videos. All those fly-ass cars, houses and bitches didn't do nothing for me but make me mad. I wanted what them niggas had, but wasn't doing shit to get it, so why keep watching them niggas shine on me? I agreed with the other workers to a certain extent. He was making a lot of money from the warehouse, but even with him bringing in that much weekly income, it still hadn't added up to what he was spending.

In jail, Rico would boast about shit he was going to get when he touched down and got his street pharmaceuticals business back popping. He was sure he was going home to take over his city and did the research on where he'd be spending his money. Rico had these foreign, custom and luxury car magazines that listed starting prices just to drive the cars off the lots that were higher than the prices of homes in my neighborhood. I'd watched Gutta pull up every day for the last two months in different whips that I watched Rico almost bust a nut over in those magazines. On Mondays, Gutta would pull up in the jet black Ranger Rover with the peanut butter inside and black and peanut butter-colored rims. Tuesday was the only day out the week when he actually looked like a warehouse worker, pulling up in his white 2002 Dodge Ram 1500 quad-cab pickup truck. Wednesday was the all-white s500 Benz that he kept all factory. If there were any additions or add-ons to his car, they were done by Mercedes-Benz themselves. Thursday was the Silver 2004 Infinite FX45 with rims on fat tires, so they protruded out on both sides. The coldest part about that whip was that Gutta was pushing the '04 version in 2003, but in my opinion, he saved the best for last. On Fridays, well not every Friday, but the ones where he was dressed to hurt niggas' feelings and to get the hos watching, he'd pull up in the all-black Maybach 62 with the rear window curtain closed. He didn't need the curtain since he had limo tint on his windows, but it did add a taste of class to it. Otherwise, on Fridays, he was driving his silver Lexus SC 430 with the top back on 23's with beats ready to blow his trunk off. All his whips had built-in phones on the dash and video surveillance in the license plates. There was no way he was cashing in like that working at this warehouse alone.

One Friday, I caught Gutta in the locker room getting shitty from head toe. The bag the suit was in read Giorgio Armani, but the box his shoes were in said Air Force Ones—white and low. Ever since the song came out the previous year, niggas had been buying the shoes two pair at a time. Gutta had on a white V-neck t-shirt, and once he threw on his Air Forces, he'd be shutting shit down. He had his long hair braided in all kinds of crazy designs, but they all lead in the same direction, to the back. His edge up was paper-cut sharp and his goatee was trimmed to perfection. The nigga didn't have a hair bump in sight. I was talking shit about his old baby-booty-face-having ass trying to look young in my head, but I guess thirty-eight wasn't really that old. It was only old to me since I was only twenty-one. He looked out the corner of his eye and caught me staring. "Do we have a problem?"

I wanted to say yes, but being jealous was a fool's reason for having beef, and I was far from foolish. I looked at him dead in the eyes and kept it real with the nigga. "However you're getting your money, I want in. A nigga tired of being hungry!"

He smiled as he put on his iced-out cufflinks. "You already on your way to getting it. Keep working hard and come in to work on time, and they'll promote you soon enough."

"Naw, I'm not talking about—"

He put his index finger in the air like we were in church to shut me up, because someone had entered the locker room. He hurriedly put on his shoes, grabbed his stuff up and walked past me. "Have a good one, youngster."

The arrogant muthafucka brushed me off without trying to hear me out. He was feeling

Dog Food

himself way too much, which would make niggas like me find a way to sit his ass down. Instead of plotting to take his shit, I made it my business to go the opposite way whenever he was around, because the urge to check the nigga could cost me my job. I hadn't been in the same room with Gutta unless there was a mandatory meeting until my ninety-day probation period was up. I had to have a one-on-one with my supervisor to determine if I'd get a seventy-five-cent pay raise or not. I almost passed up the meeting with him due to my dislike of him, but that would have been stopping my own money.

"I see you've made it ninety days and your production hours are off the chart. Look at all the overtime you've been working. Are you saving for something special?"

"Yeah," I responded, keeping shit short.

"What are you saving for if you don't mind me asking? Stacking bread like that, it gotta be something big."

"Yeah it is." I fought with myself about telling him then said fuck it. "I'm tired of living in a motel. I need my own spot, and then I'm going after my mama's old house. I'm trying to buy it before someone else does."

He looked uneasy about my response, but continued on without asking me anything else about it.

"So," he ran his eyes over my file to retrieve my name, "Demarcus Elder." He repeated it again, this time slower and questioning. "Demarcus... Elder?" I could tell he was racking his brain then he asked, "Why does your name sound so familiar? What's your daddy's name or do you have any brothers my age?"

"No, I'm the only child and I don't know shit about my daddy."

"I know that name, I'm sure I've heard it before! Did you play any high school football? I follow all the good players..." He stopped talking. I could see it in his eyes that he had figured out who I was, and I could also see he thought that I was guilty of what I had been accused of, because immediately our meeting came to an end. "I'm going to get your file over to the big boss to see what Paul decides to do, and if your raise is granted, you'll see it on your paycheck in two or three weeks. You can go back to work."

"All right." I snickered knowing he had wanted to say more.

He jumped to his feet, opened the door and made sure to let me out without shaking my hand as he had done when I first entered.

At first, I was worried about him trying to get me fired over that rape shit, but then I remember the big boss had already known about it before offering me the position. The nigga would have to deal with the fact I was there whether he liked it or not.

Demand for sheet metal was at an all-time high and production had to match it. We were called in to help the weekend workers on the Saturday following my meeting. I didn't know anyone who worked on my shift, but on Saturday I ran into two guys I had played football with. We were on rival teams but had been cool over the years because of our love for the sport. On our lunch break, we decided to play catch up. I could tell the shorter of the two, Jamal, really didn't have too much to say to me, so I started picking at him.

"What's wrong with you, Jamal? I know you're still not mad at me for dragging you like a rag doll into the end zone." I laughed and so did everybody listening in to our conversation.

"Naw, I ain't mad about that, but I know what you're mad about! You're still mad at Alabama for snatching that scholarship up from you after you raped that little girl, ole pedophile ass nigga!"

I went to jump over the table on his ass but was caught in midair by Gutta. I was taken into his office with a lot restraint

"You need to calm down! His words mean more to you than making money? Nothing that fool said should have made you fall out of character, especially when the entire world knows he ain't lying about you!" He was writing up a serious incident report while I paced around his office.

"You and the entire world don't know shit," I roared. "Neither does he! Everybody listening to the news, but ain't nobody took the time to ask me about it!"

He leaned back in his chair, still mad that I had caused a scene on his shift with other supervisors present, then said, "Here's your shot, hot head; spill it!"

I told him the story the way I explained it to Rico the day I moved into his cell, but Gutta got the extended version that included my cousin not telling me about my mother's death and having to live in a motel to survive. When I was done, he looked up at me and then started filling out the report again. When he was done, he tore off the carbon copy and handed it to me.

"You're suspended for the rest of the day. If you were still in your ninety-day probation period, you would be fired. You can't react off people's words like that, especially when you know they don't know what the fuck they're talking about. Come back Monday with your head on right."

I went storming out of the door. When I returned to work Monday, I found out that Jamal had been let go. He already had two other write-ups for similar issues and was always calling out of work and showing up late. I had killed my production numbers, knowing I was going to be monitored from that day forth. Two minutes before my twelve-hour shift was over, the Hispanic team leader, Marcos, came up to me saying, "Gutta wants you to stay and work two more hours to help our team get caught up since what you did Saturday is the reason we're behind in the first place."

"Fuck Gutta," I mumbled under my breath, but told Marcos, "All right, cool."

I ran outside and gave Bria some money and told her to go down the road to the race track and gamble for two hours since there was a casino in it and then went back to work. Dog tired didn't describe how I felt after putting in those two extra hours. I was sore and walking in slow motion to Bria's car.

"Demarcus!" I knew it was Gutta calling me, but acted like I didn't hear him. I had caught us up and had production at 10 percent already for tomorrow. If he was asking me to stay longer, he was doing it just to fuck with me.

I kept walking to the car until his hand fell on my shoulder, stopping me. "What?" I snapped, eye checking the shit out of his hand to let him know he shouldn't have touched me.

"You need to learn how to control them emotions," he said, shaking his head. "Look, if you still want to get to the money, fix your attitude and give me a call. I might just have a sales position for you." He handed me a business card that didn't have a name or any other information business cards usually have. The only thing on the card was a printed telephone number in bold font.

"A sales position? What we selling?"

"You ain't selling shit, not yet. It's a process, takes some learning and the right attitude. We'll talk more about later."

"All right," I said, losing interest and turning back toward the car.

He let me get all the way to the passenger's side door then said, "Demarcus, what do you know about the Dog Food industry?"

Immediately, all interest returned...

Chapter Eleven:
Class Is In Session

I hated to lie to Bria, but if she would've known I was meeting up for an introduction to the drug game, she would have taken it as regression. I had made so many positive strides at securing my future that she wouldn't understand why I'd be willing to risk it all for greed. I fed her a line of bullshit about production being needed at work for a few hours and asked if I could use the car.

"I don't want you dropping me off today, baby. I don't know how long they are going to keep me, and if I only have to do a few hours, I want us to stay in bed all day."

"What if you have to work a full eight or even twelve-hour shift? Then I'm wasting my Saturday indoors doing nothing. I'll just drop you off and you call me when you get off."

Nothing I said would get her to throw me her keys, because her real problem with me using her car was that I didn't have a driver's license. She'd let me drive while she rode on the passenger side, but that's as far as it went. I didn't want to argue with her about it. It was her shit, even though I paid a few of the notes on it. She just gave me confirmation that I needed to see what Gutta had in store for me so I could hurry up and get my own shit.

I had her drop me off at work then called myself a cab. He set it up for us to meet at a restaurant on Beale Street, which wasn't that far from my job anyway. When I sat down at the table next to Gutta at the blues spot, he stood up.

He paid the waitress for his drink and said, "Leave your car parked here, let's go on a walk."

It wasn't uncommon for men to walk together around Beale Street, but it was the middle of the day and the street didn't get packed until sunset. In my opinion, we looked suspect, but I didn't say shit. We chitchatted about work and why production had picked up until we made it to the riverfront's dock.

"Tell me what you know about Dog Food."

"I know it's heroin and that there are more than 1.2 two million people in the United States using it and—"

He started laughing hysterically at me and even had to walk away to pull himself back together.

"You looked the shit up online?"

"Yeah."

I didn't see the humor in me doing the research on it. I thought the more I learned about it on my own the less he'd have to teach me, but Gutta thought the shit was funny.

"Truth is, the only thing I know about it besides what I read on the internet is that it was the reason behind my aunt and uncle getting murdered when I was kid. And, you can make lots of money off the shit if you don't get caught or addicted to it."

Seriousness returned to his face. "Take mental notes, Demarcus. One, never get on the internet searching for shit like this again. If you have questions, that's what I'm here for. That internet shit is traceable and the DEA and Feds keep up with IP addresses whenever people start probing for information on that kind of shit. Make that your first and last time! Two, if you worried about getting caught, you need not apply. Scared money don't make money. I'm not saying you're supposed to be all out with the shit, but there is a right and a wrong way to go about it. I can't fuck with you if you're scared, Demarcus. A scared nigga will have me sitting behind bars."

"I ain't scared. I wouldn't be here if I was. You asked a question, and I answered it. Don't flip that shit on me," I blurted out.

"That right there brings me to my next lesson. You have to learn to respect the hand that's feeding you. I get it! You're big, bad-ass Demarcus that feels like he has to prove something to the world after the shit you've been through. But I promise you won't get a bite off my plate or the chance to lick the bitch clean without learning how to fix that attitude of yours! As a matter of fact we're done for the day."

He started walking back in the direction of the restaurant, but I didn't move. When he noticed I didn't follow him, he came back ready to talk shit.

Before he could open his mouth to form a word I said, "We're not done for the day. You had some other shit planned. I respect you and what you're saying. Respect is everything, but it goes both ways. I understand I'm an invited guest into your world, but I can only give the amount of respect I'm getting in return. As long as you remember that I'm a man and talk to me like I'm one, this shit will ride smoother than your Maybach. And niggas I really fuck with call me Dee."

He smirked and then said, "Done, Dee!"

We sat down on one of the docked boats and talked for hours. He started off with basic rules and even broke down the handling and packaging of *Dog Food*. Before we went our separate ways, he handed me a cell phone.

"This is a business-related phone only. Nobody should have this number unless I give it to them or give you the okay to do so. Business and personal shit never works out, so don't be tempted to mix the two. When this phone rings,

Dog Food

be ready to move. What are you driving around in anyways?"

I pulled back up to Bria's apartment in my used, dark blue 2001 Nissan Altima that Gutta had purchased for me. He paid cash for it, but copped it at one of those buy here, pay here lots. There was nothing flashy about the car, but it was mine and it would get me from point A to point B. He told me to take Monday off work to get my license and the car registered in my name, but when I returned to work, I needed to keep the shit the exact way it had been before he gave me the opportunity. That meant we didn't say shit to each other at the plant.

On the ride to the car lot, Gutta told me he had fucked with one other cat at the job with this heroin shit, but it blew up in his face. He said the nigga got greedy with the shit and the next thing he knew, the he was being carried away from the job in handcuffs. Although he had taken his charge without snitching on Gutta, he promised himself not to fuck with anybody else at the job. Gutta didn't know it, but I knew he was talking about Rico. Rico had told me he had been arrested on the job, because his job was his only traceable whereabouts.

Gutta confirmed it was him when he said, "The nigga was Paul's brother-in-law. He was a real country nigga from deep South Mississippi who had fell bad on his luck. I was trying to be like Red Cross and help him get back on his feet, but he wasn't used to listening to shit. He wanted to run shit his way like he did in his city. I tried to tell him that shit didn't work like that in Memphis, but he didn't want to hear it. When they arrested him, I took my vacation time off work, waiting to see when my world was going to crumble, but the nigga stayed tight-lipped about me. I'm telling you this to give you a glimpse at the chances I'm taking by fucking with you, Dee. If you trust me and listen to my words, you won't have to worry about shit."

I probably should've told him I was cool with Rico while I was locked up, but didn't want to jeopardize him deciding to fuck with me.

Bria wasn't home when I made it upstairs, so I used my key and let myself in. I tried to call her to tell her I was here, since it was my first time being in the apartment without her, but her phone kept going to voicemail. She had given me a key to use, which made me think she wouldn't mind me being here when she made it back. I sat on the couch watching TV for an hour then boredom kicked in. I started walking around, room to room, trying to find something to get into, but everything she had to occupy herself involved reading. I found Bria's ten pound dumbbells she had in the guest room and started lifting them, but they were too light to feel any impact. So, I went into my full jailhouse workout until I was covered in sweat. I had over done it and couldn't get up. I was lying there on the carpet next to the bed about to take a nap, but something under the bed caught my eye. There was a narcotics anonymous book and a three-ring spiral notebook that both looked worn out. I grabbed them and started flipping through the pages. My first thought was that neither could belong to Bria, and she probably used them to help with counseling members on her caseload, but the note book proved me wrong. There, in Bria's own handwriting, were notes she had taken from NA sessions, information from abused women counseling meetings that she had attended, and a daily diary she had kept. I flipped through the pages until one that was dated June 22, 1998, caught my full attention.

He's the DEVIL and the drug is his pitch fork!

I don't know how he found me, but he did and now my sobriety is thrown out of the window! I tried to walk away, hoping he'd suffice with just a quick hi and bye, but I should have known better. There's no way to fully be done with him while still living on this Earth. It was like he had marked his spot on me and the smell of his own scent was always traceable. This is the fourth shelter I've had to move to just to get away from him, and like all the others, he made his way here. I can't believe how it happened. I got up at 5 am like I do every morning, to take my jog in peace. When I walked out the battered women's shelter to start my morning jog, his car was parked at the building next door and he was sitting there smoking a cigarette, waiting on me. I jogged right past him and gave him a quick wave, but that didn't work. He grabbed my extended arm and started hugging and kissing on me like nothing ever happened between us.

As I was pulling away from his grasp, he starting telling me how much he missed me and how he had looked everywhere for me. He told me how he had to threaten my mama just to find out where I was. He made me all these promises about how if I went back home to my mama's house, things would get better. He'd get us our own place, help me to stay clean, and how he would never hit me again, but I knew it all was bullshit. We started arguing back and forth, and the next thing I knew, he was forcing me in the back seat of his car by my hair. I started screaming, swinging, and kicking to get him off of me then I fucked up and cut him under his eye by accident with my sobriety ring. When I went to check the gash I had put under his eye, he pinned me face down by the back of my head on to the floor with the lower half of my body still lying across the back seat. He snatched a bag out of his jacket pocket and put it under my face. It was a bag of pure, and he wouldn't let me up until I inhaled a nose full of it. All it took was for the shit to get in my system and he had me right where he wanted me. He pulled out his hardened girth and rammed it up my butt right there in the back seat of his car with his blood dripping all over the back of me. The sad part about it was I couldn't feel the pain because I was too busy trying to get another sniff out of the opened bag.

When he was done, he gave his normal threat about if I went to the police how he'd kill me, my mama, and my little sister; then threw me out his car on to the hard concrete with the bag following me. I ran down the street to the park and cleaned myself up at the lake. The cold water was bringing down my high, but I couldn't let the rest of the gram go to waste. I found a bench and sat there getting high until the bag was empty. I went back to the shelter high as a kite. I lied to all the staff saying I wasn't strong enough to go without it and was sent back here for detox. Now everybody is disappointed in me and I've lost all the alone privileges I had earned. My case manager said they were going to put me out if I did anything else and gave me two strikes for my relapsing.

Lord, help me! Why are You still protecting him? He needs to be killed for what he keeps doing to me. Why do You give him access to always find me? It's not real love God. Why don't You see that the devil doesn't know how to love? Why God? WHY!

Just when I got ready to turn the page to see what other questions she wanted to ask the Lord, Bria came in throwing her bags down onto the dining room table. I threw the book and folder back under the bed in time for her to catch me doing pushups when she walked into the guest room. It felt good to know that I wasn't the only person keeping secrets about the past in our relationship, but I knew it was my duty to be the one to bring both of our secrets to the table. Bria was addicted to cocaine? I still couldn't believe it after seeing proof of it with my own eyes. Just when you think you know a person, you find out that you really don't know shit!

Chapter Twelve: Grams or Better

"After I got my hair and nails done, I went to the department store and got you five Polo shirts, three pairs of Levis and," Bria grabbed a bag that contained a shoe box in it and handed it to me. "Open it!"

She wore an excited look on her face as I released the drawing string on the bag. Bria had brought me a fresh pair of Polo boots. They were the high-top ones that had the strap across the shoe with POLO embedded. I had told her I wanted a pair when we were on Beale Street two weeks ago and saw them on someone's feet for the first time. I couldn't have pretended like I wasn't excited if I wanted to.

"Here, go get your musty self in the shower and put this on with that Curve cologne I got ya'. I want some eye candy while I eat."

She was so happy about getting her man shit that I didn't protest. We needed to talk, but I decided to wait until we were in for the night instead of killing her joy. I got in the shower, shaved, and then took my time applying my cocoa butter. I threw on a black beater and a new pair of boxers I had sitting in a pack for nights when I slept over and then got dressed. I felt like money when I was done. When I walked into the living room to model my shit for Bria, she had a fucked-up look on her face.

"Demarcus, whose cell phone is this? I thought you said you weren't going to get one until I added you to my plan?"

The cell phone was inside my jacket's pocket, which meant Bria went snooping through my shit, or it had been ringing and caught her attention. I snatched the phone out of her hand and there were two missed calls displayed on the screen. Without hesitation, I called the number back.

"Where you at Dee? You ready to make a move with me?"

I could tell Gutta was driving his car, because I could hear traffic in the background.

"Hell yeah, where are we meeting up?"

"I'm headed to your motel. I'll be pulling up in about ten minutes to get you. Be outside."

"I'm at my girl's spot, but I'll be there in fifteen." I hung up the phone and threw my jacket on.

"Where in the fuck do you think you're going? We're supposed to be going out to eat! And who the fuck was that calling you, Demarcus?"

Dog Food

I couldn't tell her the truth, but didn't have enough time to come up with a lie to smooth shit over; I needed to bounce. "A friend from work, and we will go out to eat when I get back, baby." I reached in to kiss her on the cheek, but she stepped back.

"You think I'm dumb, don't you? All of a sudden you have friends and a cell phone that I don't even have the number to, but your 'friend' does? Tell that bitch you're on the way to give her the shit back and I'm taking you to do it!" She grabbed her car keys off the table and started putting on her shoes.

I knew it wasn't the time to tell her about the car, but I pulled out my keys, hoping she'd catch on. "There ain't no bitch, Bria! I keep telling your insecure ass that it's all about you. I'm about to meet up with my boy from work for a second, then I'll be back to pick you up. Go get ready."

When I opened the door to leave, I watched the half-full soda bottle that she had been drinking on when she came in fly over my head.

"You have the bitch picking you up from my house? Oh, hell naw. I don't know who you think you fucking with, but both of y'all will be dead if she's down there waiting on you!"

Bria ran to the living room closet and grabbed a metal baseball bat. I took off running with her right behind me. She was fast, but I was faster, especially since she slowed down when we hit the stair case and I picked up speed by taking three or four steps at a time. My car was in reverse by the time she made it to the parking lot. I rolled down my window as I was about to pass her and said,

"I love you, baby. I'll be right back. I promise!"

She said a whole lot of fucked-up shit in those few seconds, but the only ones I was able to make out were, "And you got a car! Fuck you and that bitch, Demarcus. I'm done with you!"

I hit a few blocks to make sure Bria hadn't followed me in her car then called Gutta back.

"Change of plans. Can you pick me up from the mall down the street from my motel? My gal is tripping, and I don't want to leave my car where she can get to it."

Gutta laughed then said, "Aww, you got you one of them types. All right, I'll be there in five."

When I pulled up, I circled the parking lot twice looking for Gutta, but couldn't find him. He called me as I was picking up the phone to call him.

"Turn around. That's me in the black Mustang."

I pulled up, parked, and hopped in the passenger side.

"What's up with your girl, Dee? You didn't tell her about our business arrangement did you?" he asked with concern in his voice.

Dog Food

"Hell naw, that's why she's tripping. I came home with a cell phone and a car, so now she's questioning me about an invisible bitch, but I didn't answer. Next thing I know, she's throwing soda bottles at me and chasing me out the house swinging baseball bats."

He died laughing and then ran down what I needed to do to resolve my issue.

"Do you love her or is she just a throwaway piece?"

"Naw, I love her and tried to tell that to her crazy ass as I was smashing off, but she wasn't trying to hear shit."

"How long have y'all been fucking off?"

"Four months, going on five. She's wife material, but she got secrets I need to get to the bottom of." I remembered what I had just read about her ex and drug addiction.

"So peep this, if she got secrets then you do too! Y'all haven't been together long enough or built enough trust from what it sounds like for you to be spilling your guts about what you're getting into. She may be riding with you now, but you don't know how well she'll have your back if the police get to questioning her."

He reached into his glove box and retrieved a cell phone identical to the one he gave me earlier then closed the compartment back.

"This will be your personal line. She won't know that this ain't the same cell phone she saw you with earlier. Give her this number to help calm her ass down some. When you're around her, keep your business line out of sight, but make sure you're still checking for my calls. Missed calls means missed money. You said you've been stacking bread right? How much do you have saved up?"

I did my numbers in my head. "I got like eighty-seven hundred. It would be more if I hadn't paid two of her car notes. And, I been paying thirty a night for my motel."

"Okay, so tell her you took twenty-five hundred out of that to cop the car. Wait, she don't have access to your money do she?"

"Naw, I keep my shit in a shoe box."

Gutta shook his head. "The money you got in the shoe box is from working at the plant?"

I nodded my head yes.

"Then it's clean money. Get you a bank account and have your work check direct deposited to it. It's the money you make with me you'll have to learn to stash. But if you're a fast learner like I think you are, you'll have to do better than a shoe box to hold it. We make two-fifty or better, depending on the customer, off of a gram of boy. I see I'ma have to teach yo' young ass everything!"

He jumped on the interstate and turned his music up. We passed up Jackson, Tennessee, before he spoke his next words.

Dog Food

"We're headed to Nashville to meet up with my baby brother so he can re-up. You ain't gotta do shit, because this is family, and starting out, you won't be moving this much weight. You ain't selling more than an ounce and you ain't getting out the bed for less than a gram. I got niggas walking the streets selling crumbs, but you ain't one of them. I'm bringing you along so you can watch and learn, because when the time is right, this is a trip you'll be making alone."

He turned the music back up and I grabbed my personal line and sent Bria a text.

Stop tripping baby, I love you!

Not even a minute later, she started blowing my phone up with call after call, but I sent her to voicemail every time then sent her another text. *Text me baby, I can't talk right now.*

She didn't waste any time getting shit off her chest once she read my message. She started sending these extra-long-ass texts asking me where I got the car and phone from, talking shit about if I'm fucking with another bitch, she's going to kill me, and how if I'm with the bitch when she finds me, we both will be dead.

I responded back with the story Gutta gave me to feed to her. I told her the phone was my surprise to her, because I couldn't reach her when I got off of work and that everything I was doing was to better us. I could tell she was calming down, because her next text finally indicated that she had heard what I had been saying to her.

Do you really love me? And if you do, why did you tell me for the first time driving off?

I didn't want to get hit with the baseball bat, slugger. Lol.

I love you too, daddy. Are you on your way back? I'm hungry and missing you.

No, go get you something to eat Bria, and I'll wake you up when I get back. I'll be gone longer than I thought.

Fuck you Demarcus! Don't come back. Go to your shit hole tonight. I'm going out.

I started to question her with whom. Where in the fuck was she going? Why all of sudden she want to go out? And when she planned on have her ass back? But I let it go and just responded with, *Okay beautiful, I'll sleep at my room tonight. Don't be out there doing shit that's gon' get somebody fucked up. I love you.*

She didn't respond back.

That was the longest ride I had ever been on, but Gutta was driving by the speed limit, because we were riding dirty. He assured me the trip back to Memphis wouldn't be a three and a half hour one. We pulled into this run down, full-service gas station named Max's Gas off of Dickerson road. The young white service worker came out and started pumping our gas and saying how we needed air in the driver side back tire. Once the tank was on full, he directed us to drive into the service shop attached to the gas station then lowered the doors on it once we were all the way in. Gutta popped the truck.

"James, go tell my slow-ass brother we here."

The white boy responded, "Yes sir," and then disappeared.

Gutta removed the spare tire and began rolling it to a table. He then picked it up and placed it on top. He dug inside the tire and removed some ice packs and a tall, dark-skinned nigga walked out the employee's only entrance.

"Damn, what took your ass so long? I was about to say fuck it and hit the club without you!"

"Shut up, nigga. You weren't about to do shit but wait on this money," Gutta replied, reaching out for a handshake combined with a tight hug.

"You sho' know what to say, nigga."

Gutta's brother, Orlando, was his younger but taller twin. Besides having long dreads instead of braids, they looked just alike. He had the same bubbly eyes as Gutta, a long, flat forehead and bulldog-shaped nose. He wasn't as buff as Gutta, but even with him being that tall, the nigga wouldn't be mistakenly called skinny. He was rocking a blue and white Rocawear fit with a pair of matching colored Jays. That was a major difference between the two. Gutta's money was so long that he only rocked the name brands of his clothes on the tags inside of them, and

Orlando felt the need to flaunt his. He made sure to sag enough to show that the band on his boxer brief matched his fit. He even left the Jump Man logo charm dangling from his shoes.

"What you got good for me?" Orlando asked, rubbing his hands together.

Gutta reached into the tire and pulled out two rectangular bricks as Orlando retrieved the scales from under the table.

"Fuck that, Gutta! This only reads two point two pounds nigga. I told yo' ass I needed two kilos this time."

"Stop whining, pussy!"

Gutta reached back into the tire and pulled out two more bricks and placed them on the scale. "You happy now, nigga?"

Orlando nodded his head up and down and said, "Ecstatic."

He went to the snow-white Escalade that was already parked in the garage when we pulled in and came back with a Louis Vuitton duffle bag.

"Happy birthday, nigga!"

Gutta wasn't worried about the bag that his brother gave him as a gift; it was the contents that had his attention. "Where's your counter?"

"Damn, you don't trust me?"

"Hell naw, nigga. I know who your daddy is," Gutta snapped.

"It's over there, but where's the trust at? Have I ever fucked you over before?"

Dog Food

Gutta gave him a fucked-up look then pulled out the money counter and started letting it count the loose bills while Orlando walked back to his Cadillac. He pulled out a Louis Vuitton suitbag then mouthed to me, "Watch this nigga snap."

About three minutes later, Gutta started looking around the garage for his brother. "Orlando, bring yo' ass, nigga. This shit short."

"Stop whining, pussy! The rest is in your second gift. Now can I get a thank you?"

Gutta snatched the suit bag and took a bag of money from the bottom of it. When it all added up, he turned to face his brother. "Thank you for my suit and the bag. Now where's my birthday party at?"

Chapter Thirteen:
The Battle of Right and Wrong

We rode to the club in the Escalade with Orlando, and when we pulled up, you would've thought we were celebrities. The club's owner approached the SUV and opened all of our doors for us while forcing one of his bouncers to act as a valet, instructing him to park the 'Lac.

"Welcome back to Nashville, Gutta," he said, nodding his hand and pulling him in for a hug. "We've got you setup in the VIP lounge, and it's fully stocked with your own waitress and bartender. We've made sure to only let the guests on the list Mr. Orlando provided us in, but as you can see, we have a line going all the way down the street. Word got out you were coming in town; now the whole city wants to party with you. We were wondering, since there were only a hundred people on the guest list, if you wouldn't mind us letting the public in until we reach max capacity?"

"Hell, naw! They gotta come back another night," Orlando answered before Gutta could. "I brought this bitch out for my brother!"

"Mr. Orlando, I do understand this, and I thank you again for choosing our location to hold your brother's event, but look at the lines. We can hold up to four hundred and fifty people, and if you'd be willing to change our arrangements, I'd give you and your guest the bar for free all night."

Both Orlando and Gutta started checking out the lines and, if they were seeing what I was seeing, the first fifty or so in line were nothing but beautiful women.

"Go ahead," Gutta spoke up. "But I need you to tighten up the security in the VIP for myself and my guests, and I'll also need you to get us about two hundred honey gold wings from that spot on Jefferson Street."

The club owner looked at the lines and then back at Gutta. "Sir, we have already tightened the security before making our request. Also, your brother already has caterers inside serving your guest. You can't just expect me to leave the club unattended to—"

"You heard my brother," Orlando interrupted. "If you ain't getting his wings, these muthafuckas ain't getting in!"

Dog Food

The club owner took out his phone and placed the order for the wings right in front us and then escorted us in.

The downstairs dance floor was empty, but once we made it upstairs to the VIP, the shit was packed. It took us twenty minutes just to get seated on one of the leather couches due to everybody shaking Gutta's and Orlando's hands, plus them taking the time to introduce me. I was getting showed love like I was one of their brothers. Every five minutes, I could hear bottles popping and niggas making toasts on behalf of Gutta. When the happy birthday wishes slowed down long enough for me to get a word in, I asked Gutta, "Why didn't you tell me it was your birthday? This must be your city."

"It ain't shit to me but another day when you get my age, Dee. This is Orlando's doing. But yeah, I was born and raised in Nashville. This party is going to be off the wall crazy. Make sure you enjoy it."

Gutta got up to greet some of his newly entering guests while Orlando slid down on the couch next to me. "Come take a walk with me."

When he stood to his feet, so did I. Gutta was talking with some guests when we walked by him, but he kept his eyes on us until we entered the men's room.

"Here." Orlando lifted the back of his shirt and handed me a gun. "Just in case shit pop off because my brother is back in town."

"Is he beefing with somebody?"

"Naw, Gutta don't do beefs, but all these smiling faces ain't as genuine as they seem. Nashville niggas are jealous-hearted. I'm giving you this just in case."

I put the gun on my waist but was nervous as fuck. I had never held a gun before, nor did I know how to shoot one. As I was covering the handle of the gun with my shirt, Gutta walked in and Orlando speedily walked out.

"What did my brother say to you?"

"Nothing really, he gave me a gun just in case shit pop off."

Gutta extended his hand. "Give it to me. Do you even know how to shoot one?"

I shook my head no.

"My brother ain't like me. I'm the Martin Luther King in the family and that nigga's Malcolm X. You can't get caught up with him, especially when you start making these trips alone. He thinks everywhere is a warzone, but I promise you that this club is not. Relax, everything is straight. Let's go dance with some of Nashville's finest."

The dance floor was packed and it seemed like every female I laid my eyes on was pretty, even the big girls in this bitch could get it. I danced

Dog Food

from one cutie to the next, making my way around the room. Orlando kept offering me drinks or to come upstairs and hit the blunt, but I was straight. I was on a natural high and this being my first time in a club where women had clothes on, I wanted to make sure I was sober enough to remember it.

I danced until my knees hurt. Then I made my way back upstairs to the couch, but couldn't get to it. A partition had been put in place in the area the couch was in and Orlando was acting as a guard to get around it. "Hold up, Dee. My brother back there getting him a birthday present."

"Is that Dee, Orlando? Send his flash-dancing ass back here to help me out."

Orlando moved to the side with a huge smile on his face, "Have fun!"

I didn't know what was up, but soon as I hit the corner, there was Gutta sitting on the couch, smoking a blunt with one hand, and sipping on something dark in the other. His drawls and pants were at his ankles. There were two bitches, one black and the other white, on their knees, fighting over whose mouth his dick would go in next with two more bitches standing there watching, waiting on their turns.

"Orlando is wild for this one. Two sets of head-hunting identical twins. Have a seat and help me unwrap my gifts."

"Naw man, that's all you. Enjoy your present."

"Damn Dee, the little chick back home got you bugging. Well can you at least hit the blunt with me or did she say you can't smoke either?"

I sat on the far end of the couch, turned my back to him and reached for the blunt. I don't know what he was smoking, but after two passes I was high as fuck. I pulled out my phone and called Bria, but she wasn't answering. Instead she sent me a text back saying, *I'm busy. I'll be by there to see you tomorrow!*

Busy? I started blowing her phone up, and every time she forwarded me to voicemail and then turned her phone off. Fuck it. If she wanted to play games, I would too. The weed had let Omar's words not to trust a bitch take dominance over my thoughts. I hit the blunt a few more times, then asked Orlando to get me a cup of whatever it was Gutta was drinking.

"That's the spirit, Dee. She probably out there fucking off, you might as well too."

Orlando came back with my glass of Hennessy and it was on. I didn't penetrate either one of the bitches. I knew I had pussy at home, but I killed their throats. I made both of the hos leave the club with my unborn kids floating around their digestive systems. Guilt started kicking in as my high started coming down, but it was too late to press rewind. I'd just have to treat Nashville like Vegas and let whatever happened here stay here.

Dog Food

We left the club around four without anything popping off. We sobered up at Waffle House while we ate. Then, Orlando dropped us off to get the Mustang. I fell asleep soon as we got in the car and when Gutta woke me up a little over two hours later, we were back in Memphis at my car.

"Get you a few hours of sleep, Dee, then we back at it. No road trips, but there's money to be made."

Gutta handed me five hundred dollars just for riding along with him. If the payment was that large for just riding with him, I couldn't wait to see what I'd get when I made the trip alone.

I couldn't believe it, but I actually missed my motel room. I jumped in the bed fully dressed and passed the fuck out. I woke up at one in the afternoon to Mr. Roberts banging on my door to pick me up to do the yard work and dinner.

"I'll be there in thirty minutes. Let me jump in the shower and throw some clothes on."

I wasn't in the mood to rake leaves, but Gutta told me to keep doing everything I was doing before hooking up with him. I turned the shower water on cold, and it gave me life. When I pulled up to the house, Bria's car was parked in the driveway. I tried to call when I got out the shower, but her phone was still going straight to voicemail. I raked the leaves, bagged them up, and then went in the house to clean up as I did every Sunday, but today was different. Normally,

Bria sat next to me at the table. This time, she was sitting in between the Roberts, and this was the first dinner we ate in complete silence. I didn't know what she had told her family about the night before, but the Roberts were keeping their words short and dry. I didn't realize it until I reached across the table to grab another dinner roll, but Bria was rocking a hickey the size of a quarter on her neck.

"What the fuck is that?"

Everyone looked up from the table except for Bria. She continued to eat, pretending she didn't know who I was talking to.

"Bria!"

She looked at me when I called her name and said, "What Demarcus?"

"What the fuck is that on the side of your neck?"

Mrs. Roberts said something about having a sweet potato pie in the oven and got up, with Mr. Roberts volunteering to help her with it. I waited until the kitchen door closed before standing up to take a closer look. As I stared at it, I noticed Bria had a slight smile on her face.

"Oh, you think this shit is funny?"

"I don't know what you're talking about Demarcus, but did you have fun with your new friend last night?"

Dog Food

"You know exactly what I'm talking about. I'm talking about that hickey you got on your fucking neck!"

She was playing games with me; that's why her ass decided to wear that strapless top, to throw the shit in my face.

"What the fuck did you do last night or should I say who did you do?"

"Fuck you Demarcus. Don't question me until you've checked yourself first!"

We went back and forth about it until Mr. Roberts came out the kitchen handing me a plate and asking me to leave.

I jumped in my car and smashed off. Fuck Bria!

Chapter Fourteen:
Back to Good

I had made fifteen hundred dollars in three days of working for Gutta, and when I got to work Tuesday, I wasn't feeling manual labor anymore. Between thinking about Bria's ho ass and noticing how my high production numbers allowed other niggas room to slack, I walked out that bitch soon as my eight hours were done.

I tried to get Bria off my mind but couldn't shake the fact that she had fucked off on me. I knew she was guilty by how she was acting now. She hadn't tried to call or text me at all. The thought of her laid up with a new nigga sent me driving in her direction. When I got to the door, I decided not to knock and used my key so if she was in there fucking off, I could catch her in the act. When I opened the door, she was curled up on the couch under a blanket watching the news.

"Put my key on the table and get the fuck out Demarcus!" She sat up and threw the blanket off.

"That nigga must be on his way over here, huh?"

"What nigga?"

"The nigga that has been putting hickeys all over my girl's neck. You know what nigga I'm talking about!"

She made her way over to me then cocked her head to the side.

"You're talking about that hickey? The one I got from my flatiron hitting my neck? That's the hickey that got your ass switching up on me and talking to me like I'm a ho?"

The same spot that caught my attention Sunday at dinner now was a black burn mark. I almost felt like shit about wrongly accusing her then I thought about the text she sent saying she was busy.

"I see yo' little burn, but what was you doing Saturday night that had your ass too busy to answer my calls. Then you said you'll be by to see me tomorrow. What's up with that shit?"

"Oh my God, Demarcus!"

She snatched her phone, dialed a number, and then put her phone on speaker.

"Hey Tee-Tee, I'm sorry to bug you—"

"Who the fuck is Tee-Tee?" I yelled, interrupting her conversation.

She cut her eyes at me then finished, "Like I was saying, I'm sorry to have bugged you, but can you please tell Demarcus what we did Saturday night to the wee hours in the morning?"

"Hey Demarcus! You should've come over here too. Lord knows we could have used the help. We went up in that attic to get the Christmas decorations since I like to put them up on Thanksgiving and I had about ten years' worth of junk we had to go through. There was boxes of lights brand new, still in the box, that I don't remember buying, and gifts I was supposed to give out from years ago. We had our hands full!"

Mrs. Roberts kept going on about what they found in the attic until Bria finally cut her off.

"Thank you, Tee-Tee. I'll be by to check on you tomorrow. I love you."

"I love you too, baby, but Bria, make sure this is the last time you call me to prove your whereabouts. If you don't have trust, you don't have nothing. I learned many years ago that the person who's accusing the next of doing wrong is usually the one doing all the wrong in the first place. They're reacting off of their own guilt from whatever it was that they had no business doing. Don't let nobody point the finger at you without making them look at the direction them three folded fingers are pointing in!"

Without her being straightforward and saying it, Mrs. Robert had just told Bria that I was the one doing wrong and Bria took an earful of what her aunt had told her.

"You know my whereabouts, now tell me about yours!"

I wasn't expecting the shit to flip on me like this. I was sure Bria had fucked off on me less than an hour ago, now I had all the proof that she hadn't. But what about her not answering my call Sunday? Before I opened my mouth to ask the question I already knew the answer. Bria was at church.

"Spill it, Demarcus! Where were you? Because when I left my auntie's house at one that morning, I had the office let me into your room. I fell asleep and woke up at six to come home and get ready for church. So I know you stayed out all night. Who the fuck were you with?"

I didn't know what to do and my eyes searched the room for the answer, but all I found was proof that I had broken Bria's heart. She had a pound of chocolate candy on her coffee table, a gallon of cookie dough ice cream with a table spoon stuck in it, a picture of us on Beale Street sitting next to it, and she was wearing one of my dirty shirts. I was on the verge of making a confession then the truth came out my mouth.

"One of my co-workers invited me to his birthday party. I didn't have a clue that his party was going to be in Nashville until we were almost in Jackson. The party was over around four, and then we went to Waffle House while he sobered up enough to drive us back. I made it back to my room at ten minutes to seven and went to sleep until your uncle came knocking."

"Is that right? Call the birthday boy up and prove it like I did!"

Dog Food

I couldn't call Gutta, this was personal business and he already told me he didn't want Bria knowing shit about him. I tried to think of a way out of it, then I asked to use her phone. She had the internet on it, so I looked up the number to the club and dialed it. I put the phone on speaker just as she had done.

"Thank you for calling Club Pleasure, this is Ted. How can I help you?"

I didn't know that the owner's name was Ted, but I knew it was him by his squeaky girlish voice.

"Hi Ted, this is Dee, the guy who came to the party Saturday with Orlando."

"Oh yes, how are you my friend?"

"I'm good. I was just telling a friend of mine how your club is the best one Nashville has to offer, so she could book an event with you. I was trying to figure out what time your club closed, because I couldn't remember if we had stayed to closing or if we left before."

"Oh no, Dee, you guys left at closing. We shut things down around three, but we don't close until four."

"That's what I needed to know, thanks!"

I hung up before he could say anything that would get me in trouble. Before I could get in Bria's ass for wrongly accusing me, she was already wrapping her arms around my neck and kissing my lips.

"I'm sorry, daddy. You were just acting weird. The phone and car thing without telling me you were getting either threw me off. Promise me you'll keep me in the loop from this point on."

"I'm sorry too, baby, and I promise to let you know shit beforehand."

I picked her up and carried her to the bed, thanking God with every step for getting me out of this one. Just when I got ready to lay her down and reward her for keeping what belonged to me as mine, my phone started ringing. Not my personal line, but the business one. I didn't answer it, knowing if I did we'd be right back to arguing, so I decided to please her with my tongue then make a break for it.

"Can you keep it wet for me until I get back?" I asked after feeling her thighs tighten around my face for the third time.

"What? Where are you going now?"

She unwrapped her legs from around my head and scooted her bottom away from my face.

"Look at the time, baby. I left work because you were on my mind. I still have another three hours to do."

She looked at her alarm clock and realized I was telling the truth. She went in to the bathroom attached to her bedroom and returned with a soapy wash rag.

"Well clean up before you go back."

Dog Food

I hit her with a bedroom smile. "Naw, I'm going to leave your scent on my face for motivation"

I leaned in to kiss her goodbye and she pushed my face back with her hands. "I don't eat pussy; you do!"

****

I called Gutta when I made it down to my car. He didn't answer, but I noticed he left a voice message.

"I see you left once you put in your eight. No need to put all that extra time in no more, right? You're fucking up! Hit me back."

No matter what I said or did, Gutta always found a way to find fault. Now I know why Rico was doing his shit his own way; there were too many rules. I'd follow the ones that made sense, but all the extra ones had to go. While I was listening to his voice message, he must have tried to call me back, because there was a new message from him.

"Come by the house, the big one."

I busted a U-turn and jumped on the interstate. Gutta's house, the one he actually lived in, was about thirty minutes from Bria's house. He was ducked off in the cut right outside city limits. His closest neighbor lived about a mile down the road. It was like the nigga lived on a secluded island, minus the surrounding water.

I knocked on the door, but there was no answer. I tried ringing the doorbell, no answer again, so I called him.

"Dee, are you deaf? I've been yelling come in, nigga. It's open."

I walked in the living room, expecting for Gutta to be on the couch since he said he was yelling come in, but this fool was in the back of the house in his bedroom. I started talking shit walking down the hall to him.

"How did you expect me to hear you telling me to come in when you're two miles away from the front door? You got a bull horn back here? No, let me guess. You got a microphone attached to your bed that's connected to surround sound, and you thought the volume was up, didn't you nigga?"

I opened the door to find Gutta lying stomach down on the floor next to his bed with his face cocked toward the door. His eyes were open, but they were bloodshot like he hadn't slept in days. I was going to shoot a drunken joke at him, thinking his current state was alcohol-related, and then I saw the big piece of gauze taped to his arm. He didn't have a shirt or shoes on, just a pair of jeans and socks. There wasn't any blood visible besides what had seeped through the gauze and he didn't look hurt, but I could tell by the way he wasn't moving that he wasn't on the floor purposely. He closed his eyes and turned his head to look away from me before talking.

"Dee, I need you to help me get back on the bed, man."

I aided him without question.

Chapter Fifteen: Hustling Backwards

I learned that nothing was going to stop Gutta from getting to the money, not even kidney failure. Although he had passed out from being dead tired after dialysis, the only thing on his mind was his money. He quickly ran down his medical history to me about how kidney failure ran in his family and how he'd been waiting on a donor for close to three years. He explained how he felt after the treatments and then quickly got in my ass about changing things up.

"You broke a rule today, Dee! You weren't supposed to switch nothing up. You've been working twelve-hour shifts since you started at the plant. You think niggas ain't gone notice the change?"

"I didn't have a choice but to switch it up. When I get off of work, I go straight to my girl's house. How am I supposed to get to the money without her noticing it? If I can't use those extra four hours to serve and have her thinking I'm still at work, I can't hustle!"

He used his elbows to move his weight around so he could sit up. "That's when you get at me.

It's only one other nigga at the plant racking in overtime every day. If you would have hollered at me, I could have made an announcement that overtime is only given out when needed! What happens when you have to hit the road though? Maybe I chose the wrong nigga to fuck with. If you can't control your bitch..."

"Watch yo' mouth, nigga. We already discussed that respect shit."

Gutta saw I wasn't playing when it came to calling my girl out of her name and apologized. "What's your plan, Dee? I need to know if you're reliable or if I need to hire somebody else that can get shit done."

"I got this! All you need to worry about, Gutta, is announcing that overtime shit at work. Everything else is on me."

"Cool."

He pointed at his closet and said, "Get that brick out the refrigerator. It's time for a promotion."

That drop was all it took for me to prove myself to Gutta. After that, the smallest package I moved was an ounce. I noticed he kept my bites limited to those four hours that I was supposed to be working, for Bria's sake. With six months under my belt, I felt like a true street pharmacist. Without Gutta's blessings, I found a way to make a little extra money on the side by selling tourniquets and boxes of needles to dealers. That was a trick I learned from moving weight back and forth to Nashville with Orlando. Gutta had made me commander-in-chief over his stash spots, and I made sure niggas were running a tight shift under my command. My money was right, and I had saved enough to reach all my goals.

When the alarm clock went off on Monday morning, a smile fell across my face. I wasn't going back to work, ever! I showered, emptied my safe, and then went to the bank and withdrew everything in my savings account. I had three hundred and fifty thousand dollars in my backpack, and I was headed straight to my mama's house to get the number of the realtor off the sign in the yard. Once I closed the deal with him and the contractor I was going to hire to fix the house up, I was headed to get Bria an engagement ring. There would be no more of us living in separate houses, and as soon as she said yes, we would start working on our first child. I wore the smile on my face all the way to the house. Then, my smile instantly disappeared.

When I pulled into the drive way, the 'for sale' sign was gone and the yard was full of workers fixing the place up. I jumped out the car and started talking to the closest nigga in front of me, but he didn't speak any English. He pointed me in the direction of someone who did.

"Who bought this house?"

He spoke enough English to be able to answer my questions.

"I don't know. We got the contract two weeks ago. Whoever it was, paid big money to have it ready for move-in in a month. Maybe if you come back then you can find out."

"Oh, I'll be back!"

That shit threw a monkey wrench in my plans. I couldn't go buy a 2005 whip without knowing how much I was going to have to pay this nigga to sell me the house he purchased and fixed up. I couldn't propose to Bria without being able to show her proof that I could provide for her, and I wasn't about to be stuck at work for eight hours a day when I needed to grind harder to get more money to offer the owner of the house a deal he couldn't resist. I grabbed the last three bricks I had and hit the interstate to Nashville. If there was anybody who could help me flip the money in record time, it was Orlando.

I didn't worry about Bria wondering where I was, because when my road trips became more frequent, I lied to her and said I was promoted to a driver at work. I told her some routes were in the area, but others could take me as far north as Michigan, West as Cali, and south as Florida. She was straight as long as I checked in while I was on the road.

Over the months, I learned another difference between Orlando and Gutta. Gutta was more

Dog Food

subtle about getting his money, and Orlando was all out with it. Whatever it took to watch the paper pile up, Orlando was with it. He had started fucking with some niggas in Atlanta on this Dog Food shit, and I wanted in. He said they'd buy up everything he came with, and they always wanted more. I ran down my situation to Orlando when I made it to Nashville, and four hours later, we were checking into our hotel in Atlanta.

"We're meeting up with those niggas tomorrow night at this strip club downtown. My connect said we didn't give him enough notice on getting a full kilo, but he'd have the money for us tomorrow."

I didn't care if he needed an extra day to get his money up as long as he sent me home empty-handed. I grabbed five grand out the back pack to get me something to wear for the meeting tomorrow night and then threw it in the closet. I wasn't worried about Orlando getting to it, because we had one of those two-bedroom suites, and we both had our own room.

I went to the Lenox Square Mall and picked out a navy blue sports jacket, jeans and boat shoes from Ralph Lauren's summer collection. It was the end of May, and Georgia was already scorching hot. I went to the club sockless with a thin, white V-neck on that only Gutta would acknowledge as stylish.

The club was packed with underground rappers and ballers. These niggas sat at tables and booths cliqued up. You could tell by long distance mugs who didn't fuck with who. I wasn't here to check out niggas. The hos in here were too bad not to give them my full attention anyway. Atlanta's strippers ran laps around the ones I saw on my eighteenth birthday in Memphis. The strippers in Memphis were cornbread fed and judging by how thick and solid these hos were, you could tell they got full on steaks and potatoes. Asses roamed free like the strip club was a farm full of horses and donkeys. I peeped a bowlegged black stallion with her eyes on me and urged her to come my way with my finger.

"Let me get a private."

She licked her full, peach-colored Georgia lips, swung all twenty inches or better of her sewed-in hair over her right shoulder and said, "It took you long enough! I got the perfect spot."

She took me upstairs and pulled back a red curtain. Sitting on the red velvet couch were Orlando and two other niggas making the drop. I came in just in time to watch the money and product switch hands.

"This is my nigga, Dee. He's the nigga next to the nigga. Whatever y'all need, he will make sure to supply." Orlando introduced me to the others.

Dog Food

"What's good with you, Dee? I'm Trae and this my right-hand man, Blue. Tell me you brought more than this with you?"

I shook both of their hands while shaking my head no and sat down. "I can bring some more this way in a day or two. I just need to know what you're trying to get. It ain't shit to drive it back out here to you."

Blue gave Trae a weird look before saying, "We'll get at Orlando when we're ready."

I hadn't noticed it, but the bitch that brought me up stairs had left and was now making her way back.

"Is y'all done yet, Trae? Y'all fucking up my private," she said, grabbing my hand, so I wouldn't exit when everyone else did.

When the room was clear, Fire went straight to work. She was on my lap naked, popping her shit slow, moving her body like a snake, and showing me just how flexible she was as she wrapped her ankles around the back of her head, exposing her thick-lipped pussy. I was enjoying the show, but something about the scene had a déjà vu feeling to it.

"This ain't the only kinda private I give, daddy." She grabbed my hand and rammed it in her pussy. "If you want to know what I really feel like, this is just a sample," she said while squeezing her pussy muscles as tight as she could around my three fingers and making it pulsate to the beat of the music. "Just tell me where you're staying tonight, and Fire will be there!"

"Like that?" I asked.

"You better know it!"

I removed my fingers out of her shit and wiped them across her nipples. Like a cat to a bowl of milk, she licked her juices away then cleaned my fingers off with her mouth. My pants woke up, ready to tear into her ass, but I wouldn't fuck up on Bria twice. My second head didn't want me to, but I pushed the freaky bitch off my lap.

"I'm good." Then I dug in my pockets and made one thousand dollars rain on her ass as she sat on the carpeted floor looking up at me like I had lost my mind.

I went downstairs and Orlando was sitting with Trae and Blue in front of the main stage. He motioned for me to step away with him.

"I put the money in the dashboard. Why don't you take it back to the room, so we won't be here with all these bands on us. I'll take a cab back to the room in an hour. I'm just finishing up some other business with these niggas."

I took the keys from him and left. About an hour and half later, Orlando came in with Fire tucked under his arm.

"You straight?" I asked.

Dog Food

He looked her body up and down with lust in his eyes and shook his head yes. "I'm about to be," he said while kissing her on the neck.

I cut the living room TV off and rolled me a blunt. Half way through smoking it, the sound of the headboard slamming against the wall and Fire screaming like Orlando was beating the brakes off her caused me to turn the TV back on with the volume on high.

"Hit that shit, 'Lando!" I said to myself, laughing.

The sound of Fire's moans sent my pants standing sky high. I wished Bria was here with me. I started rubbing my man the way Bria would to let me know she wanted some. My hand didn't feel as good as her, but my imagination was a muthafucka. I freed my man and spit on my hands to replicate the feeling of her mouth. As I stroked him, I replayed the nasty shit Bria said whenever she made me her lollipop and then came knocks on the door, right before I could give her a taste of my cream filling.

I thought it might have been room service, so I went to the peep hole with my man swinging to finish the job after I sent them off, but it was Trae and Blue. I tucked him away and wiped my hand on my shirt before opening door.

"What's up? Orlando is in the room handling some business. Y'all can have a seat on the couch while I go get him." I turned my back and took a step toward Orlando's room.

The sound of one being put in the chamber sent me turning around to find Trae holding his pistol in my face and Blue nudging me with an assault rifle. "Naw, you have a seat nigga. We'll go get Orlando."

Chapter Sixteen:
Cut Off

Trae forced me to the couch and kept me there at gunpoint while Blue went to retrieve Orlando. A few seconds later, Orlando came crawling into the room naked with Fire kicking him in the ass, her gun pointed at him. I could hear Blue rambling through shit in Orlando's room.

"Y'all just sit here quiet and don't try shit, and I promise y'all make it through shit alive." Trae was talking to both of us, but kept his eyes on Orlando.

"Nigga, I thought y'all could be trusted. I heard y'all niggas in the A weren't nothing but some bitches—"

Fire hit Orlando in his mouth before he could get the rest of his words out. "My brother ain't no bitch, and it's y'all ratchet-ass Nashville niggas that's with the shit. Payback is muthafucka, ain't it?"

"I don't know what you're talking about," Orlando said, not sounding one bit believable.

The little bitch had some hands on her, because within seconds, Orlando's lip swelled up like an allergic reaction. Trae pointed his gun at Orlando, and Fire switched places with him, now pointing hers at me.

"You know what she's talking about nigga. You get that one for free. The next slick shit out of your mouth gon' cost you more than the money you robbed us for, bitch," Trae told Orlando.

About two minutes later, Blue came out of Orlando's room, giving Trae an inventory of what he had found.

"Thirteen hundred dollars and an ounce of 'dro. That's all this nigga had!"

"Nigga search again. I know he got more than that on him! Matter fact, I'll go look."

Blue came up and pointed his gun at Orlando. Trae put his hands on the top of the rifle and pushed the barrel down until it was an inch away from Orlando's exposed dick.

"Blue, if this nigga says anything, send him back to Nashville neutered. He's been trying to talk shit with his ho ass."

I learned from seeing how easily Fire had hit Orlando not to say shit. I kept my eyes on Fire's ass, because this bitch was the true definition of why bitches can't be trusted. I guess my stares were making her uncomfortable, because she put the gun closer to my head and said, "I should shoot your ass for shoving your nasty ass fingers up my pussy like I'm some kinda ho."

Dog Food

Blue reached over and popped me in my head with the handle of his rifle. I fell over, feeling dazed, with a knot growing where the rifle had met with my head.

"You touched my bitch? You better hope I let yo' ass live!"

Fire smiled like him calling her his bitch was an honor, when she should have taken it as a sign of disrespect.

"I didn't! She grabbed my—"

Fire's fist shut my mouth as Trae came out of Orlando's room empty-handed. He went into mine, and three minutes later he walked out holding my backpack and some sheets. "Bingo! Tie these niggas up while I count this money."

Blue and Fire tied us up then laid us on our stomachs on the floor.

"That's what I'm talking about, Blue! This nigga was walking around with three hundred and forty grand in an old ass backpack. Man, and throw a cover over that nigga. Y'all got his ass in the air like a bitch."

Fire and Blue started kissing and hugging like they had hit the lottery. The room was silent for a long-ass time, which gave me time to think. I'd rather be dead than to leave Atlanta with everything I had saved up gone. I called out to Trae, trying to think of a plan to be freed long enough to fight for what was mine, but he didn't respond.

"You hear me nigga. I got to pee," I yelled, but still heard nothing.

"What the fuck were you doing with all that motherfucking money on you, Dee? And them niggas been gone."

I couldn't answer Orlando, because my tears and dry throat wouldn't allow me too. I cried like a baby and Orlando started screaming out for help. He must have screamed for three hours straight, but no one ever came. We weren't freed until the hotel staff came to put us out at check-out time the next morning.

When they saw us tied up, one of the staff members ran back out to call the police as a young, black guy untied us.

"Look, we can't talk to the police, because we can't tell them we were robbed for drugs and drug money, you feel me? Hurry up and untie us so we can get dressed and leave before they get here."

The guy seemed to understand what Orlando had said to him and put some pep in his step to free us. We were pulling out the hotel's parking lot as the police were pulling in.

Orlando smashed off, making call after call, telling people what had happened to us the night before. He was already making plans to avenge the incident as soon as he and his boys got together. I couldn't do shit but cry. I didn't have anybody to avenge the shit that happened to me, nor could I offer any help, because I hadn't dealt with anything like this before. The only real nigga I had in my life was Rico, but he had been released, and I didn't have a way to contact him. When I got my crying at bay, I dialed Gutta's number.

"Who the fuck you calling?" Orlando asked, with his phone still mounted on his ear.

"Gutta."

He dropped his phone on his lap and covered the mouth piece with his hand.

"Hang up. You can't tell that nigga shit about what happened. I got this!"

"But what about his money?" I asked.

"Gutta's money is in the dashboard. The only money them niggas got was them funky ass thirteen I had in my pocket and the loot you had in your bag. Give Gutta his shit, and he'll pay you like he always does. Don't mention none of this to him!"

I cleared his number off my screen and put the phone down. I felt like I was dead inside. No money, no job, and there was nothing I could do about either. I fell asleep with a heavy heart. I woke up when we made it to Chattanooga with my phone ringing back to back on my lap.

"Hello?" I said.

"What's up with you, Dee?" It was Gutta.

"Nothing much," I said while tapping Orlando to let him know it was his brother on the line.

"Remember, don't tell his ass shit!" Orlando whispered to me.

"What's up with you? Why you ain't at work?" I asked Gutta, trying to play shit cool.

"I was about to ask you the same. You sure you straight?"

"Yeah, I'm good!"

He cleared his throat. "I heard something different! If you and my brother plan on keeping shit a secret, tell him not to call my goons for help!"

I didn't respond back to Gutta. I handed Orlando the phone, so he could deal with it. I don't know what Gutta said to him, but Orlando ran down the whole situation and included the backpack full of money. He gave me a fucked-up look then handed me back the phone.

"You are the dumbest nigga I ever fucked with, you know that Dee? Bring me my money and I'm done fucking with you."

"Then pay me in Dog Food instead of cash for making this move for you, and I'll get back on my feet by myself!" I snapped.

"I'm not fucking with you. What part of that you not understanding? You don't have any clientele. Them are my bites. Bring me every last dime of my shit and I'll give you your money for making the move, and then we done."

"You can't do me like this Gutta. I don't have shit. Paul left me a message saying I'm fired for no call no show yesterday. After all the shit I've been doing for you, you're just going to leave me for dead like this?" I decided to play the personal side of things, hoping to make Gutta change his mind.

"I didn't leave you for dead when I found you on the floor, did I?" I whispered, trying not to let Orlando hear me.

Gutta didn't say shit at first. Then he answered, "Naw, you didn't leave me for dead, but I ain't fucking with you like that no more. You broke too many rules. I told you don't switch shit up and you did. I told you not to quit your job, you did that too, and I told you to be careful with fucking with my brother and you didn't listen. Your days of working for me are over. What I will do for you is holler at Paul and tell him you called me saying your ass was in a car accident and would be out for two or three days, but you better have your ass here at six tomorrow, ready to put in twelve hours. That's all I'm willing to do for you!"

He hung up and meant what he said. When I made it back to Memphis, I called him to meet with him to bring him his money, but he had already arranged for me to drop it off at one of his stash houses. He told me to take five thousand out of it for myself, leave both of my phones there, and don't even look his way at work. He cut me off without any regrets.

Chapter Seventeen:
You Can't Burn Bridges

Months had flown by, and I hadn't seen Gutta not one time at the plant. He didn't even do my yearly review, leaving it for Paul to handle. I was promoted to Shift Supervisor, which was strange, because from what I knew, that was Gutta's position. I started asking around if anyone had seen Gutta, and Marco told me he was pushing papers from home now. He requested a desk job due to medical reasons, and it was approved. I felt bad for the nigga, but I wouldn't trade making twenty-one dollars an hour in exchange for his health, not after the way the nigga cut me off.

I had given up on chasing down my mama's house for the owner and looked at as, if God wanted me to have it, He would have made it easier for me to get. I got Bria an engagement ring, proposed, and she said yes. So I moved in with her and took over all the bills. We'd find us another house and work together to get it. Bria told me awhile back that I had to crawl before I could walk, and that's exactly what I would do. I had finished making the upcoming week's schedule and was about to call it a night when my office phone rang.

"Sheet Metal Crafting, this is Demarcus speaking."

"Dee, this is Gutta. Can you come pick me up from the Methodist hospital? These muthafuckas won't release me unless I got my own ride."

"Hell naw, nigga, we ain't cool!"

I hung up the phone then headed out the door to go pick him up. I told him no to give him a taste of what it feels like to have somebody cut you off when you need them.

When I made it to the hospital, Gutta was sitting on the bed, fully dressed with his bags packed. "You ready to go or are you waiting on your sponge bath?"

He reached over the bed and grabbed the talk button and said, "Tell Nurse Debra I'm ready for discharge. My ride is here."

Gutta didn't look the same at all. His hair had thinned out to the point you could see his scalp through his thin ponytail. He had to have lost fifty pounds or more, and his dialysis port was now in his neck. When we made it to his house, I had to carry him in, and he asked to be put on his couch. "Look, Demarcus, I just want to say thank you for—"

"You don't have to thank me for shit. If anything, I owe you thanks and an apology. You were right. I fucked up my own money. I can't blame you for cutting me off."

We shook hands then Gutta confirmed nothing had changed about him but his health. "Go look in my safe and take out fifty thousand. I need you to make a run to Mississippi with Orlando for me to re-up my stash houses. I'm putting you in charge from here on out. You still got your motel room?"

I explained my new living situation as we waited on Orlando to arrive.

"I'm not ready for your girl to know what's up yet, Dee. Get you another motel room and I'll pay for it. You're going to be the legs and I'll be the brains in this shit."

I met Orlando in the driveway like Gutta requested, because he didn't want his brother seeing him fucked up. On the ride to Mississippi, Orlando told me how they had caught Blue leaving the strip club with Fire and smoked their asses while they were getting out the car in their drive way. He said a week later, they ran up in the church while the funeral was being held and took Trae's ass out.

"Y'all killed the nigga in a church with his family watching?"

"You sound disappointed about the shit. Where else was we supposed to catch the nigga slipping at? He knew he was next and kept his killers with him. We knew the church house was probably the only place he felt safe, so we caught the nigga in there slipping."

"In the church house though?"

Orlando didn't know how deep I was into the church growing up, so he didn't understand why it affected me the way it did. I didn't respect Uncle Leroy deciding to pimp out of it, and I refused to respect Orlando for making the house of prayer a murder scene. I knew the nigga was shady but didn't know how much. I vowed to keep my eyes on the nigga from now on. If he didn't give a fuck about God, why would he give a fuck about me, or his brother for that matter?

"You could have caught that nigga another time. That sin is too great to be forgiven for! If you don't fear God, your days in that flesh are numbered."

He shrugged his shoulders like my words meant nothing to him, and said, "I ain't worried about no nigga, including Him. If you're feeling some type away about it then pray for me then, nigga."

I didn't say shit else to him about it the rest of the ride there, but I had to make sure he knew I didn't respect his decision. I couldn't believe I made it to the drop with a dead nigga sitting next to me. I had to fight with not throwing his anti-Christ ass out on the interstate and keep driving. My mood was bad, too bad to go and conduct business. But when we made it to Latimer,

Mississippi, I pulled up at the drop just in time to catch Rico's ass leaving the hotel, duffle bagged up.

"Does your parole officer know what you got in them bags boy?" I said, walking up behind Rico.

He looked over his shoulder at me while he was in the trunk of his Jaguar.

"Who the fuck is that?" he said, reaching for what I knew was a gun.

I quickly announced myself. "Damn Rico, you don't recognize your little brother, Demarcus, when you see him nigga?"

He dropped whatever it was in his hand, closed his trunk, and ran over to me for an open armed hug.

"Damn, Dee, look at you boy! You getting old on me. Looks like you've been eating good out here!"

"I can say the same for you, pushing that 2006 Jaguar."

"What's up Rico?" Orlando said, moving in for a hand shake and a quick hug.

I didn't have to ask how they knew each other, because if Rico worked for Gutta, I was sure he sent him on those trips back and forth to Nashville as he had done me. Rico didn't seem too thrilled about his reunion with Orlando, but he didn't say shit. He shook his hand and hugged him back.

Dog Food

"Guess y'all going to see King David too, huh?" Rico asked, and we both nodded our heads yes.

We didn't have time for a full reunion since this was a business trip, but we exchanged numbers and Rico promised to make his way to Memphis next month to celebrate my twenty-fourth birthday with me.

Orlando had made a negative name for himself, because King David wore a disappointed look on his face when he saw him. He even made sure to ask me not to bring Orlando back the next I came, and I assured him I wouldn't.   I made it my number one priority to ask Gutta what was up with Orlando when I made it back. I didn't see it until now, but he was a nigga I definitely didn't need to be fucking with.

"He's greedy. He's fucked over everybody he's done business with in the past, including me. If he wasn't blood, he would have been dead. That shit that happened to y'all in Atlanta was pure retaliation from him setting up those niggas to get robbed when they came to Nashville. Orlando thinks the shit he does is untraceable, but everything always links back to him. When I had the nigga from Mississippi on my payroll that I told you about—"

"You're talking about Rico, right?" I interrupted Gutta, but with him putting me in charge over his whole operation, I felt it was time to put everything out in the open. "I was locked up with Rico. He's the one who told me about the plant and to holler at Paul when I got out. We ran into the nigga re-upping with King David last night. I wanted to tell you that I knew the nigga but first wanted to hear what you thought of him, like if I can trust the nigga or not."

"You can trust him. He's a real nigga, just hardheaded like you. We made a lot of money together and, to be real with you, he's the one who put me up on game about my brother cheating me out my money and all the other side shit Orlando is into." Gutta laughed then said, "So the nigga found out who my supplier is and plugged himself. He was smarter than I gave him credit for, with his country ass."

We sat and talked about Rico and Orlando, and then Gutta moved the conversation to himself. "I don't live in a fantasy world, Dee, and I'm not going to pretend that I'm going to live forever. My kidneys stopped functioning on their own three years ago, and my health has gone downhill ever since. I watch niggas play with their kids in the park and listen to you talk about starting a family with your girl and regret not having that myself. I've lived my life married to money with my cars as my children. I've never trusted a soul until I met you. If I was to die right now, everything would go to my mama who has dementia. That means it will all be Orlando's. My daddy has been serving twenty years on his life sentence, and he ain't never touching down."

Gutta reached over to his coffee table, grabbed his blunt out the ash tray, hit it three times, and passed it to me before continuing. "I'd burn this shit to ashes before letting Orlando have it. What I'm trying to say is you won't need Dog Food to help you make it through life, Dee, because when I'm gone, I'm leaving everything to you. The house, cars, money, and anything else I got is yours. All I ask of you is to send me to glory in style. I want to be buried in Nashville—"

"I'm not trying to hear all that, Gutta; you ain't going anywhere, no time soon."

He stopped me in my tracks. "Yes I am, and sooner than you think. I took myself off that bullshit donor list. You gotta have money to get a higher spot on the list, and in this situation, my drug money doesn't mean shit. I'm a single warehouse worker with no kids and no real reason for preservation. Everything is a factor when they find matches. When I'm gone, Demarcus, move in here. Sell whatever product you have left and get out the game. You won't need it making twenty-one dollars an hour at the plant. You'll have everything you need in life from me."

"Whatever you say, Gutta."

"I'm serious Dee," he said while yawning.

I took the covers off his bed and covered him up with it. I put the television remote and cell phone in arm's reach then bounced. If Gutta was a man of his word, my days in the heroin business were numbered.

Chapter Eighteen:
I Wasn't Ready

My twenty-fourth birthday was less than a week away, and I still hadn't secured any plans, but whatever I came up with would involve spending it with Rico and Bria. Bria was talking about going out for dinner or maybe a Mississippi river boat gambling trip, but I wasn't feeling either one. I didn't know what I wanted to do, but neither one of her suggestions sparked me.

I asked Rico what he wanted to do and he said, "It's whatever nigga. Just know whatever you decide the shit's on me!"

I was trying to come up with a plan for my birthday on my way back to the hotel in Biloxi. I had to pick up Orlando after I had re-upped with King David. Orlando didn't like the idea of me meeting up with Gutta's connect without him, but I had to respect King David's request. Hell, I didn't want him coming along with me after knowing his true colors, but Gutta said the trip was too dangerous for me to make alone. I knew the twenty-one-questions session would start as soon as I picked the nigga up.

"Did you watch the nigga weigh it out in front of you? You made sure nobody was following you, right? That nigga didn't try to make any side deals with you that's gone fuck my brother up did he? I don't understand why King David wanted you to come alone. My brother doesn't even re-up with the nigga by himself! You gotta watch out for shit like that. It might be time for my brother to start fucking with somebody else. That Jamaican nigga has always been a snake, and I don't think he should be trusted anymore."

I didn't answer Orlando's questions. He knew why King David didn't want him coming better than I did. If I had broken it down to Orlando that I knew the reason why King David didn't want me to bring him, it would have let the information Gutta gave me slip. I wasn't going to be the cause for the niggas falling out. Gutta was too sick to be using the little energy he did have on his cut-throat-ass brother, and I wasn't going to be responsible for the usage. Orlando liked to play dumb about a lot of shit he did, and I wasn't the nigga to pretend to fall for it. If he wanted to know why King David didn't want him coming with me, he'd have to ask the nigga himself.

We loaded up all four stash houses with product when we made it back, and I took a mental inventory of what was still needed. Like always, Orlando made him some extra money off the dealers by convincing them to buy their

Dog Food

needles and baggies from him. It wasn't like he was stealing any of Gutta's money, but he sure was making a few dollars off his brother's enterprise. Everything Orlando did around me made it hard for me to be able to keep fucking with the nigga, but there was business that had to be done. Once we made sure every stash house was straight, we made our way downtown to kick it. Orlando couldn't make it back for my birthday and wanted us to celebrate tonight. I hadn't invited him to spend my day with me, but he felt like it was mandatory he did. I was tired and was in need of some sleep, but Orlando wasn't having it.

"You'll sleep when you're dead nigga. We're partying tonight!"

Beale Street was packed and jumping like it was every weekend. The ladies were dressed to impress, and the alcohol was flowing up and down the streets. We went inside one of the bars on the strip and danced with every woman in the building. Orlando had purchased a round for everybody in the club, making sure they all knew it was my birthday. Within an hour and a half, I was sloppy drunk. I had made six trips to the restroom to drain my weasel and hadn't heard my cell phone ring or beep from missed calls until this last trip.

The calls were from Tony, one of my generals who I left in charge of the stash house in Orange

Mound. I had just given him work, so there wasn't a reason for him to be calling. I called him back, but the phone went straight to voicemail. I checked the message he left that said it was two minutes long, but I couldn't hear shit but rambling, like his phone had called me by accident in his pocket. I sat there and listened to the message in its entirety then I heard the reason for his call. Right before the call ended, I heard gunshots ring out. I ran out the bathroom, snatched up Orlando, and headed to the car. I played the message on speaker phone for Orlando.

"I don't hear shit, Dee."

"Shut up and keep listening!"

When the gunshots went off, Orlando looked up at me then said, "Floor this bitch!"

I didn't give a fuck about the police being hot in the city. I had to get there to figure out what happened fast. We pulled up at the two-bedroom, one-bathroom house, and Tony's car was still parked in the driveway. By visual inspection, everything looked intact. I couldn't see any bullet holes outside the house, nor were the police outside taping it off like it was a crime scene. The lights were on inside and, like usual, I could hear Tony's music blasting in the house.

I knocked on the door. Orlando pointed out the door frame to me. It had been kicked in and the wood was cracked where the door's lock would be secured in it. Orlando used his shirt to turn the knob on the door and it opened. As soon as we walked in, we knew something wasn't right, because the house was empty. It was one of Gutta's rules that someone had to always command the houses, twenty-four-seven, while product was in it.

I went to check the bedroom, because that's where we kept the Dog Food. I turned the knob with my shirt as Orlando had, and saw that all the floor boards had been pulled up. The ice packs were still there, but not one package of heroin could be found. The room wasn't fucked up like somebody went digging to find the spot, but like whoever opened it knew exactly where to look.

"Dee, come here!"

Orlando was standing with one foot in the hall and his other was in the bathroom. He kept turning his head from the bathroom to the hallway as I made my way up. I could hear the shower running and noticed steam coming into the hallway. With the front of the shower closed by the curtain to prevent the water from hitting the floor, I could see two fully dressed bodies stacked up, one on top of the other, and a tub full of blood. I pushed the curtain open with my arm and there was Tony and another nigga I couldn't make out under him, dead. From what I could tell, Tony had been shot through his head and chest by something big. He had burn marks around his right eye and the left eye ball was missing. I couldn't see how the other corpse had met his death, but I could see that three of his fingers were burnt off to the knuckle. I grab a towel off the rack, lifted the toilet lid, and threw up all the alcohol I had consumed. I ran into the hallway to get myself together and to get some fresh air.

"The Dog Food we just dropped off is gone!" I said to Orlando as he made his way back up the hallway.

"They tortured those niggas in the kitchen. There's blood all over the stove and an eyeball stuck on a screwdriver sitting on the kitchen's counter top."

Orlando's stomach was stronger than mine. He didn't throw up, but he kept jerking his head like he would. He went and looked at the lifted floor boards in the bedroom then made his way back into the bathroom. He took the cell phones from both bodies and two grams of dog food out of Tony's pocket.

"Take this," he said, giving me the two grams.

I put them in my pants pocket.

"We gotta take anything that these niggas might have on them that will link shit back to my brother. I'm taking what the boy he had in his pocket too, because when the police notifies their families, I don't want his mama heartbroken to find out what the reason behind it was. Grab the ice packs from the floor and put the boards back up, and let's bounce!"

We moved quickly, and when we walked out we had the hoods of our jackets on. We made sure nobody saw what we looked like and that nobody was outside watching us drive away. As a precaution, Orlando said he would take my car to the chop shop and sell it in Nashville. Just because we didn't see anybody watching didn't mean they weren't. When we were ten minutes away from Gutta's house, Orlando stopped at a payphone and told the police to go check out the address then hung up. I don't know if he was paranoid, or if it was a part of him being precautious, but he made sure to wipe the payphone down before jumping back in the car.

"That shit was an inside job. Who else is normally at the house with Tony?"

I named a few people I'd seen with him when I made drops, and Orlando said to keep an eye on them. You can call it paranoia if you want to, but something told me that this shit was the beginning to a whole lot of other shit. I had a feeling that the inside person was Orlando. He had an ample amount of time to plan the robbery and murders out while he sat in the hotel as I made the pickup. I wanted to give him the benefit of the doubt, but I had never dealt with shit like this. Gutta had never prepared me for what would happen if shit went bad. There wasn't a backup or emergency plan in place from what I knew. I didn't know if this was the first time shit had gone sour like this for him or if there was a strategic method to handle it, but I'd ask as soon as we made it to him.

Gutta told me he didn't want his brother seeing him down like this, but it was an emergency and I didn't have a choice. I opened the door with the key and let Orlando walk in first.

"Gutta, wake up nigga. One of your stash houses just got hit!" Orlando said while shaking the shit out of Gutta. "This nigga knocked out!"

I sat down at the end of the couch by Gutta's feet and broke down crying. Gutta wasn't asleep, my mentor was dead.

Chapter Nineteen:
When It All Falls Down

The days that followed all seemed gray and lifeless. The beautiful fall days of November looked like they had been filled with April showers. I couldn't think straight and was fucking up left and right, but my biggest fuck up wasn't discovered until the night before my birthday and the eve of Gutta's funeral.

I had just made it back home from Nashville after approving the final touches on Gutta's funeral arrangements. I turned my key and opened the door, but the chain was preventing me from gaining entrance.

"Bria, take the chain off the door, baby."

"No, let me die in peace!"

The word die made me push the door open 'til the chain snapped. Bria was sitting in the dark in front the living room's coffee table with candles lit everywhere. In front of her was a needle, a belt that was looped to act as a tourniquet, a bent up metal spoon, and a gun.

"I don't know if I should let the heroin finish killing me, or if I should just shoot myself in the head to speed up the process."

She wasn't going to have the option of shooting herself, because I grabbed the gun, took the bullets out of it, and tucked in my pants. "What the fuck is wrong with you?"

Looking into her eyes, I could see she was high as a kite. Her lips were dry and ashy, and she was holding her arm out stiff, as if her high would immediately come down if she moved her arm.

"Nothing is wrong with me. I gave y'all exactly what you wanted, you child molester!"

"What the fuck are you talking about Bria?"

"You know what I'm talking about! You raped a little girl and went to jail for it for two years and hid it from me. Why would you think you could hide something like that from your almost-wife?"

My eyes shot down to her finger and the engagement ring was gone.

"How did he find me? How did you always know who I was? That was smart of him to use you to get me to fall in love then trap me with heroin. Call him, Demarcus! Tell him I'm high and he can come rape me in my ass like he always does. Tell him I'll go back home with him. I'm tired of running." She turned her face toward the door then yelled, "I give up; you win!"

"Bria, I'm confused, baby! Why are you shooting up? I thought the reason you were in rehab was cocaine. Why are you fucking with heroin?"

"So, he told you about me being in and out of rehab? Then he should have told you what it was for, unless you were dumb enough to believe I smoked crack."

She started looking around the room paranoid. I took a step toward her to calm her down and she pulled out a turkey carving knife from in between the couch cushions.

"Baby, I don't know him, and you're scaring me. Put the knife down!"

"Why stand in my face and lie Demarcus? I know you know him!"

"I swear I don't, baby!"

She raised the knife and slit her right wrist before I could stop her. I picked her up like a sack of potatoes and threw her over my shoulder.

"Put me down and let me die! This is what y'all want anyways."

Blood flew everywhere as I carried her to Gutta's pickup truck that I had been driving since Orlando had disposed of my car.

"Let me die, Demarcus. I can't keep going through this with y'all!" Her voice had lost its strength and she was losing a lot of blood.

When I pulled into the hospital, Bria's eyes were closed. "Somebody help us!"

Everyone sitting at the desk in the emergency room came running out. They threw Bria on a gurney and disappeared with her. I sat at the hospital for four hours waiting on information on her, but nobody would tell me shit. I went outside to hit the blunt I had in the pickup truck and saw Mr. Roberts chain smoking cigarettes in the parking lot.

"Is she okay? They won't tell me shit! She lost so much blood, and I didn't know she was addicted to heroin—"

"Demarcus!" Mr. Roberts yelled to shut me up, so I could listen to him. "Bria lost a lot of blood, but they are taking good care of her. She'll be fine. She'll be on suicide watch for a while. Then, we will get her back in rehab but..." He placed both hands on my shoulders and shook his head from left to right.

"This thing y'all got going on is over! We've worked too hard to keep her clean and in church. If you have this type of negative effect on her, I can't let this keep going on. When I told her about your past this morning, I assumed after all this time y'all have been fooling around, you would have been a man and told her. I didn't know you were out here selling heroin or this relationship, engagement, or whatever you want to call it would have never happened. I'm disappointed in you, son! You got out of jail and turned into Omar. How do you think your mama feels, looking down at you from Heaven?"

He put out his cigarette and headed to the hospital entrance.

Dog Food

"Mama would know I turned into a man and I'm not worried about the thoughts of the dead. You act like it's okay for her to keep a secret like this from me. It's cool that she didn't tell me she was a recovering addict to you, huh? Nobody thought to tell me that I was falling in love with a needle pusher!"

"Go home, Demarcus. You're not wanted or welcomed here!"

I walked past him. "You can't keep me from her. That's damn near my wife lying in that hospital bed. Call the police, because I'm not going anywhere."

He ran up behind me and snatched me up by my shirt. "The police want to know where she got the heroin from. If you don't want to be sitting behind bars tonight, I suggest you leave!"

"Are you threatening me Mr. Roberts?"

"No, Demarcus. I'm stating a fact." His eyes softened some then he said, "Please go home, and I'll call you later to give you an update on her. She's using the little energy she has to lie to protect you. I'll call you later!"

Later never came, and when I called the hospital asking for her, they said no one was there with that name. Rico made it in around ten o'clock that night to ride with me to the funeral the next morning. We stayed at Gutta's house. Well, after everything was cleared up, I guess the truth was that we stayed at my house. We smoked and drank all night, telling each other stories about Gutta's big heart. Neither of us could sleep, and I had more than Gutta's death on my mind. I told Rico what happened between me and Bria, and how I was grieving over both of my losses.

Rico didn't give any feedback on my situation with Bria, but he ran down his relationship with Orlando. "I know you got a heavy heart right now, Dee, and now ain't the time to be discussing this, but Orlando's name is all over that stash house hit. The nigga did it before with King David and his stash house. Gutta had to pay King David's goons off to spare his brother's life. That's why we meet at the hotel now. Everybody in that muthafucka, including the front desk staff, is on King David's payroll, and every one of them fucks is heated at all times. A lot of niggas don't know it, but walking into that hotel is like walking into a death trap. I'm not going back home 'til we get to the bottom of this stash house shit, and I know for certain you straight."

The funeral was exactly the way Gutta had wanted it. Due to an issue with the embalming of his body, his casket had to be closed, but everything else was perfect. The church was packed, and I was shocked to see King David in attendance and gooned up. What shocked me the most was that Orlando didn't attend his brother's home-going. Rico said he heard some of

Dog Food

the family talking about how Orlando was pissed at his brother for leaving everything to me, and to show how mad he was, Orlando decided not to attend.

I told Rico about Orlando killing that nigga in Atlanta at his sister's funeral and King David put his goons on alert. Orlando was the biggest bitch I had ever met for not being here to lay his brother and the hand that fed him to rest. If I found out he had anything to do with the stash house being hit, he'd be in a grave plot turning in to dust next to his brother.

I held the repast at a hotel in Nashville off of West End, and I made sure to hire Gutta's favorite wing spot as one of the caterers. They had a huge projector screen playing pictures of Gutta and his close family members on repeat. I didn't know any of Gutta's relatives, but they all showed me the utmost respect and thanked me for sending him home in style. I got lost in the slideshow as people began departing and didn't realize who had come to sit next to me.

"It's good to see you again, Dee!" Lord King looked ten years older since the last time I had seen him. And although seeing him brought back the memories of that fucked-up night at the strip club, I was happy to see him.

I shook his hand then hugged him tight. "Thanks man. I never got a chance to thank you for getting me that lawyer. If it wasn't for you, I'd probably still be locked up!"

"That was nothing. No thanks needed. Your mama asked me to help, so I did what I could."

"I thought Omar got you to do it?"

He laughed and shook his head no. "Me and your mama grew up together, and she had got me out of a lot of shit in the past. She didn't understand why I chose the path that I did. When my shit took flight, I tried to give her a few dollars to show my appreciation and she threw them back at me." He laughed then said, "I was happy to finally be able to return the favor."

"My mama," I said, trying hard not to choke up, "she passed away while I was locked up."

Grief fell across his face, and I could tell he didn't know. "I'm sorry to hear that, Dee. I had visited her in the hospital when Omar said she was sick, but she told me she was doing better and would be getting out soon. I asked was she going home, and she said they were sending her to a nursing home. Something told me she wasn't being honest, but you know your mama; she'd keep a secret to her grave."

The talk of my mama was wearing on my heart since I still hadn't gone out to her grave to show my respect, so I changed the subject. "So, you knew Gutta?"

He laughed. "Yeah I knew Mr. Fresh-to-Death. He was the only nigga in Memphis to give me a run for my money. We crossed paths a few times, seeing we were in the same line of business, but never had any beef. I knew what sides of town was his, and he knew which ones were mine. The world just lost one of the few good niggas it had left in it. How did you know him?"

I thought about lying and saying we were just co-workers, but I had no reason to hide anything from Lord King and let him in.

"I worked for him at both of his jobs, if you know what I mean. He was a good man and a man of his word. He left me everything he owned, but I'm going to sell his house. It doesn't feel right being in it after he died there. You know what I'm saying? I'm going to try and find out who owns my mama's house and buy it from them."

Lord King had a look of confusion on his face, but didn't say anything. I didn't really care about Omar, but I thought I should ask about him anyway. "How's Omar doing?"

"Omar is Omar, man. He's still running in the streets with me. He don't think I know it, but he's trying to sit me down and take over what's mine. He's making moves without my blessings and leaving me to clean up after him. I'm getting too old for this shit, Dee, but I can't retire knowing a hot head will be left in charge."

He shook my hand, gave me another hug, and left as quietly as he had walked up. I don't know what it was about Lord King, but I'd always liked and respected him. I hoped he wasn't going to leave Omar to run his shit.

Chapter Twenty:
Pieces of a Broken Puzzle

Bria's whereabouts were still unknown, and the Roberts weren't returning any of my calls. I didn't want to give up on the love of my life, but she was showing signs that she had given up on me. Two months had passed since she had taken the knife to her arm, and I still hadn't heard anything from her. I went by her apartment, but there were new tenants living in it. I called her job, and they said she quit. I left messages on her cell phone, but she had never returned any of them. I tried to take my focus off finding her, and it worked as long as I was making moves with Rico, but Monday through Friday, when I was at work, sitting in my office alone, she ran laps around my mind.

I should have told her about my past and forced her to tell me about hers, but it was too late for that now. Everything was out in the open. I had to live with the way it all hit the air.

Rico had gone home two weeks ago to check on his kids and make sure his business was intact. He didn't know it, but his company was my therapy. He said I should keep trapping for a few more months just to find someone to leave in charge after I retired, but he knew I'd be choosing him. I picked him up after meeting with King David on one of my final two trips and we headed back to Memphis. I was back to staying in my motel room, but whenever Rico came in town, we'd stay at Gutta's old house.

"Dee, I found out from talks on the street that Orlando didn't have shit to do with that stash house being hit. It was done by some Memphis niggas. I'm still working on finding out what Memphis niggas though," Rico said while rolling up a blunt.

I cared about the stash house being robbed and my workers being killed, but I had asked Rico to do some other investigating for me. The mission I sent him on was a greater priority to me than the stash house being hit. "Did you find out who owns the house at the address I gave you?"

"Yeah, I did." He dug in his pocket and pulled out a folded up piece of paper. "The owner of the house name is Sharon Elder. She paid it off last year sometime."

"Naw nigga, you looked up the wrong information. Sharon Elder is my mama."

He looked at the paper again and said, "Look nigga, that's the name the tax assessors gave me. If you don't believe me, call them yourself."

I snatched the number out of his hand and called them. I was told the same information Rico had given me. After going back and forth with the chick on the phone, she gave me the bank's info to speak with them directly.

"Thank you for holding, Mr. Elder. I apologize for your hold. I just wanted to make sure the information I was giving you was correct." I could hear the guy from the bank flipping through some papers as he spoke.

"It seems that the payments on the house went eight months without being paid, and we did attempt to sell it, but Mrs. Elder... You said that's your mother, correct?"

"Yes, she's my mama," I said for the umpteenth time.

"Sorry, I just have to make sure. Well, it seems like your mother came in and caught her notes up last year and even paid the house off. She is indeed the true owner of the house. Is there anything else I can help you with?"

"Hell yeah there is! Can you explain to me how a dead woman paid a house off from the grave?"

The mortgage officer began to stumble over his words like he was shooting me a line of bullshit.

"Mr. Elder, I can't say... Well, I don't think it's possible if she was already deceased for her to have purchased the house, because signatures are required. I do know there are times when a person dies and the bank comes in to take it and the executor of the will may step in and pay the house off."

I could hear him flip through the pages faster. "I don't see any executor information in this documentation but wait, what did you say your name was?"

He was pissing me off. I told this nigga my name one too many times already. I blew the frustration out of my mouth then hit Rico's blunt before answering. "Demarcus Elder. D-E-M-A—"

"Yes sir, thank you," he said, stopping me from spelling out my name. "I actually see in the notes that there was a will in place that listed you as the beneficiary." He got quiet as the pages kept turning then found what he'd been looking for. "There are notes in here about your visit to our bank. It seems that you came in the bank a while back to request a name change and you became upset with one of the loan officers because we couldn't change the name on the deed out of yours. If you give me a second, I can track down the will and get a copy of the deed to see if—"

"Two minutes ago you told me you didn't have shit. Now you're saying something different? Fuck it. I'm on my way up there, and I don't want to talk with your dumb ass when I get there!"

I hung the phone up in the clown's face. Rico looked lost and I didn't know how to explain what

Dog Food

I heard, because the nigga on phone couldn't explain it to me. I told Rico to go re-up the stash houses for me while I went down to the bank to see what was up.

The bank was packed, but when I walked in, I was greeted by this real cute, dark brown chick who knew my name.

"Nice seeing you again, Mr. Elder. If you give me a second to grab your files, I can explain it all to you."

She was flirting with me like we had flirted before, but I didn't recall ever meeting her. During my senior year of high school, I had girls hounding me from everywhere, so I chopped up our encounter to one that might have occurred back in those days.

"Okay. Let's get started."

Teresa, who worked over the deeds and titles department at the bank, broke down the whole situation to me. To sum it up, my mama got behind on payments, she died, the bank put the house up for sale, the will left the house to me, and someone came in and paid off the five year balance that was left.

"How could y'all just let anybody come in here and pretend to be me?"

"Pretend to be you? I signed you over the deed myself and even gave you my telephone number, which you never used. What happened to you making me your girl and spoiling the shit out of me?"

"You didn't sign me over shit!" I retorted. "And if I asked for the number, I would have used it."

She handed me a folder then crossed her eyes and her arms with a stank attitude. The first page was a copy of the deed in my name, and the next was a copy of my now expired state ID. It was the one I had before I went to jail.

"Now stop lying, Demarcus; the proof is all there. You even told me about your side hustle and how you helped manage the strip club. How do I know all of that if we've never met?"

"Can you make me a copy of everything in this folder, please? I'm sorry I never called you."

She put a smile on her face, and I did too, but we were smiling for two different reasons. Although Omar thought he was sneaking to get my mama's house, the truth of the matter was the house was mine. He put all that money into it to fix it up and was about to get his ass thrown out in the streets. I tried to call Rico while Teresa made my copies, but he wasn't answering.

"When should I expect a call?" she said, handing me her number first, then the copies.

"I'm going to hit you up tonight and, if you act right, we going out to celebrate."

"Celebrate what?"

Dog Food

With a smile as big and bright as hers, I said, "My takeover."

It felt good to know that I was about to throw Omar's ass out in the street and there wasn't shit he could do about it. I knew he wouldn't leave without a fight, but I was ready for the match. My foot fell heavy on the gas pedal as I visualized putting Omar on his back. Blue lights cut on behind me as Rico called me back.

"Ay nigga, I'm going to hit you right back. The police are pulling me over for speeding."

I took the ticket with a smile on my face and even thanked the officer for keeping Memphis' streets safe. But it seemed like every time I got some good news, bad news came. It seemed like the bad always outweighed the good.

I called Rico back, expecting to hear he was done with the stash houses. Instead, he hit me with some bullshit that wiped the smile off of my face.

"I made it all the way to Raleigh before I realized I left the scales at the stash spot in Frayser. When I pulled back up, Spank and them other cats were getting robbed by four niggas. I ducked off behind the house 'til they were done. Now I'm following them niggas to see where they're going."

"Is Spank okay?" I asked

"Yeah, they gave them the Dog Food and those niggas tied them up. Go get Spank and then call me to see where I am, Dee."

I busted a U-turn then hit the gas. Spank was tied up with newspapers stuffed in his mouth. I removed the newspapers as I untied him.

"Dee, a nigga ain't never been this happy to see you. How did you know we got hit?"

"Rico left his scales, and when he pulled up, he saw them niggas tying y'all up. He's following them now; then I'm meeting him to see where they went."

"Take me with you. Them niggas about to meet their maker!"

He rubbed his wrists for a second then grabbed a chair out the kitchen and climbed into the attic. He came back down with more guns and bullets than Rambo.

"Rico said you weren't by yourself when they robbed you. Where is everybody else at?"

"It was me, Boo, and this little flip bitch we were about to run. They took the bitch with them and made Boo show them where the other stash spots where at. Boo ain't no bitch, so he's probably dead by now."

"You think the bitch was in on it?"

Spank shrugged his shoulders. "I don't know. These hos can't be trusted, but she's chilled with us before and I know where her mama stays. If she did have something to do with the shit, I'll put one in her mama's head."

He was mad, but I knew he meant what he said. Robbing and killing went hand in hand when dealing with this drug shit, but I wasn't for it. I didn't want to sound like a bitch about it, but I couldn't sit back and let innocent people die.

"Don't do shit unless I give you the blessings to, Spank. We can't run this shit like war. This is an enterprise, and we're going to handle this shit like a game of chess. Every move we make from now on will be smart, young nigga."

"Cool, it's however you want to do this shit, Dee."

His words made me realize that I was in charge. I was feeling the respect given to my words. He didn't question me nor did he object. He understood he was under my command. I was the boss and he knew it, but how long would I be able to hide the fact that I was a bitch when it came to this gunplay shit? An army is only as strong as its leader. Knowing that, it was time to beast up!

Chapter Twenty One:
The Takeover

Rico wasn't as familiar with Memphis city streets like I was, and the directions he gave me were all fucked up.

"They dropped two niggas and a bitch off at a house on Deerskin, but the nigga driving is going somewhere off of Raines. I'm two cars back, following his ass now. I'll text you the address whenever he stops."

Rico didn't know it, but the streets he was shooting off to me were in the area of Memphis I had grown up in, Westwood. With Spank on my passenger side, we made it to Third Street and Raines in less than ten minutes. Rico didn't send the text message with the address like he said he would, so I pulled into a pharmacy's parking lot and called him for an update. "What's the address, Rico, or are you still following him?"

"Naw, he pulled into a driveway and used a key to get into the house. I'm thinking this is where the nigga lives. I couldn't see the address, but I know how to get back to the house. It's this little market called Royal King that I passed on

Raines and Westmont. Meet me there in ten minutes."

"I'm down the street. I'll be there in two!"

We pulled in and parked. Three minutes later, Rico had done the same and jumped in the car with us, putting Spank in the back seat.

"Bust this left at the stop sign and make a right at the next one."

Rico had directed me to Bluebell Cove and pointed out my mama's house.

"That's the nigga's car right there."

I pulled into the Robert's yard, trying not to make shit obvious that we were staking out the house. For good measure, I got out the car and knocked on the door.

"What are you doing nigga?" Rico asked as I kept knocking, hoping someone would answer.

I checked the back yard and both of the Roberts' cars were gone, but Bria's car was hiding under a blanket near the shed. I took a few steps back to see if I could tell if anyone was upstairs, and looking down on me from Adam's bedroom window with the lights on was Bria. When our eyes met, she quickly moved away and turned out the lights. I didn't know if she was on some fuck shit or not, so I jogged back to the car and sped off.

"What was all that about, Dee?" Rico asked, sounding irritated.

Dog Food

I looked at Spank through the rearview mirror and instructed him to get my cigar box from underneath the front passenger seat.

"Roll up, Spank. I got some wild ass shit to tell y'all."

I hit a few blocks then pulled in Westwood Community Center and parked. Spank had fired up the blunt and passed it to Rico, but I didn't speak a word until the weed was good in my system.

"The house that bitch ass-nigga pulled into is the same house I grew up in. I don't think the nigga knows who he's robbing, but we're getting robbed by my bitch ass cousin, Omar."

"What?" they both said in unison.

"That's the house I told you to look up for me, Rico. That's my mama's house. When I went to find out about it, the banker said my cousin came in there and paid it off since it was left to me in my mama's will. That bitch nigga thought he could just walk in the bank and forge some shit in my name then sign the house over to himself. But the shit didn't work out like that. It's my name on that muthafuckin' deed, which makes the house mine!"

"Dee, this shit don't sound one hundred, my nigga. You're saying we getting robbed by the same cousin who didn't tell you your mama died, and the same cousin that got you caught up with that rape shit, but you drive off instead of letting us run in there and off that nigga? Help me understand why we sitting at the park getting fucking high instead of running in on that nigga and making him break bread?"

"That's what I'm talking about, Rico," Spanked joined in. "Those niggas just robbed me at gunpoint. They killed Tony, and Boo is probably dead at this point, too. What are we waiting for, Dee?"

"We waiting to play this shit out smart! That's my house, and I can go in and out of it as I fucking please. Y'all gotta fuck with me on this one. That's my first and only cousin, my mama's nephew, and I know everything about that nigga. I know how he thinks, who the nigga is working for, and where they push their weight at. I know where the nigga is laying his head, how to get in his shit, and where he goes when he's trying to relax. Remember what I told you earlier Spank, we move smart like a game of chess. But I feel where y'all coming from. We won't get that nigga yet, but there's some other shit we can handle while we over here though. You and Rico ready to put in some work before we call it a night?"

"Hell yeah," they harmonized.

I needed them to put my plan in motion, but they were both thirsty for blood and I had no choice but to let them get some after what happened to my workers. We went back on Deerskin, and I waited in the car as they went beast mode in the house. I didn't hear any shooting, but Spank came out with the barrel of his nine still smoking, and Rico was toting large bags full of shit. We didn't say a word until they emptied the bags out on my bed at the motel room.

"We got them niggas for guns, money, weed, cocaine, and for half the heroin they stole from us," Spank said excitedly.

Then Rico spoke up. "That ain't no replacement for Tony or Boo's life though. This shit here don't add up to what they took from us."

"They killed Boo?"

They nodded their heads yes then Spank said, "Yeah, they killed him. Then I killed the nigga who admitted to doing the shit! Rest in peace, Boo!"

We stayed silent for a moment, then Rico asked what our next move was.

"I'm going to setup a meeting with the nigga in charge over there and see if we can arrange for some kind of peace treaty."

"Peace treaty? And if that shit don't work?" Spank asked, mad that I would even attempt to make peace with those niggas.

"Then it's all-out war, ain't gone be no more talking. It's blood over mines!"

After dropping Rico and Spank off, I went to the riverfront where Gutta had taken me. I wanted to feel his presence and come up with the right way to approach Lord King. He wasn't the average nigga, he was a kingpin, and coming at him sideways or too soft would only make matters worse. I wanted to come at him the way Gutta would have.

After mapping out my next movements, I drove the Maybach to the strip club and pulled up to the valet.

"Good evening, sir. Thank you for choosing us for your live entertainment needs."

"I'm not coming in, but I need you to do me a favor."

I gave him a thousand dollars and an envelope with a letter inside to give to Lord King telling him to call me with no signature.

"I'm sorry sir, but I don't know of any Lord King."

"Yes you do; stop playing stupid. I know like you do that he owns this joint. I got four more thousand to make sure he gets this letter."

"This isn't a bomb or nothing dangerous is it?" he asked, inspecting the envelope and placing it to his ear to check for a tick-tock.

"Naw, he's an old friend of mine, and if you make sure he gets it tonight, I'll make sure he gives you a thank-you gift as well."

He tucked the envelope inside of his vest and reached for the other four grand.

"I'll take it straight to him, sir!"

Dog Food

I watched him run inside the strip club and then drove down the street and parked at a fast food restaurant. Within ten minutes, Lord King was calling me.

"Who is this?" he asked.

"This is Dee, Lord King. Don't say my name if you're with Omar right now."

"Hey Calvin, what's up with you, man?" Lord King said, confirming Omar was nearby.

"Can you meet me alone in ten minutes at the soul food spot around the corner from the club? We need to talk."

"Is there something wrong?"

"There's a lot of shit wrong, but this phone ain't gone do it any justice. My problems aren't with you. It's with your bitch-ass employee."

"I'll be there in ten, Calvin."

Lord King pulled up in an all-black Aston Martin with tinted windows.

I got out my car and walked over to his.

"Gutta loved that Maybach. You make sure you're taking care of it, Dee. What's this meeting about anyways?"

"Omar, he's been fucking me over for years, but now the nigga is fucking up my money, and I can't have that, Lord King. I know he's working for you, so I'm bringing it to you to make the shit stop."

He fidgeted in his seat and then popped the seat belt off and got comfortable. "That was you that hit Deerskin early tonight, wasn't it?"

I nodded my head yes.

"You know you took out one of my faithful employees. I'm not worried about the shit y'all took, that was crumbs, but I'll never run across another nigga as loyal as Mouse again. We shouldn't even be talking after what y'all did."

"I'm sorry for your loss, but you of all people know that retaliation is a muthafucka. Two of my stash houses have been robbed by your people, and three of my loyal workers have been killed behind it. Is this your way of saying you want war with us?"

My stomach turned as I said the words, but if I showed any signs of weakness, I would lose the battle before it started. He dug in his pocket and pulled out a cigarette. He never lit it. It just sat on the left side of his lip.

"You need a light?"

"Naw, I don't smoke anymore. It's the hand-to-mouth motion I still crave. Fuck the nicotine. That shit will kill you," he said. "Look Dee, and this conversation don't leave this car. Like I told you at the funeral, Omar is running the show now. I told him I don't do business like this, but he's determined to knock out anybody in the city who's pushing Boy, he's greedy! You're better off trying to talk to your cousin by yourself and work this thing out. I'm sure if he knew it was you, he'd ease up, and I know we got a place for you on team if you want to join."

"You gon' sit here and insult me when you know I got my own organization? I came to you because there's no talking when it comes to me and Omar. He's done some unforgivable shit to me in the past, and if I can't get you to put your dog back on his leash then you need prepare to lose a lot of money and more faithful employees like that bitch, Mouse."

"Is that a threat, Demarcus? You call me to meet you to threaten me? Is that how Gutta taught you to handle shit?"

"Gutta is dead and left me in charge of his empire. I don't like war, but I'm not comfortable with losing money either. Get Omar's ass in line or there's going to be bloodshed."

I reached for the handle on the door, but Lord King hit the locks on it. My heart went racing, but I showed no signs of fear.

"Dee, Omar put me on the hunt to find out who hit the Deerskin spot. If I tell him it was you, you wouldn't live past tomorrow. You know I owe your mama, so I won't tell him it was you, but you need to figure out your exit plan from the drug game. I can't stop him from coming after you. I can only prolong it. I promised your mama that I would never do anything to hurt you or her, and I'm a man of my word. I don't doubt that you're ready for war, but you're not dealing with a nigga who has a full deck. Omar been through a lot of fucked-up shit in his life, and that nigga ain't right in the head. I can't promise you that a meeting with him will turn into a happy family reunion if you get at him with the same bullshit you're bringing to me. You see, I'm going to let you live even though I should shoot your head off your shoulders for thinking you could threaten me. Omar ain't gone give you the same pass!"

"Let me out your car."

Lord King hesitated and then hit the unlock button.

Before I closed the door all the way, I stuck my head back in the car and said, "Then I guess this means war!"

Chapter Twenty Two: The New Civil War

I didn't trust Lord King, but I did believe him when he said that he wouldn't let Omar know it was me he was beefing with. He didn't know the details of my problems with my cousin, but something made him understand them. He might have felt obligated to keep me safe by the promise he had made to my mama. I don't know, but whatever made him decide not to tell Omar, I appreciated it. Talking to him gave me the confirmation I had been looking for regarding whether or not Omar had Lord King's blessing to make his moves. But what in the fuck did that shit mean? Omar was still sinning in the name of the Lord—Lord King that is—and with every sin came a set of consequences that I was ready to dish out. I wasn't trying to play God biblically, but I wanted Omar to know that all his blessings would come through me. Until he did right by me, I'd make sure the nigga wouldn't eat.

When I started working for Gutta, my goal was to get enough money to buy what I wanted and get the fuck out of the game. I didn't see or want a future in this heroin shit. I wasn't in the shit to take over anybody's hustle, but the thrill of shutting Omar down helped to change my goals and create new ones. Seeking vengeance with the broken heart Bria had caused turned me into someone I never knew I could be. I was becoming a monster, the good guy turned bad guy, and I yearned to be looked upon as the evil villain in this dog food industry. Not only did I want to take over Omar's share of Lord King's enterprise, but my goal was also to knock Lord King's old ass out the picture too. Sources had told Rico that Omar was knocking out everybody selling Dog Food in Memphis, so his beef wasn't just with me. He wanted to be the only distributor in the city and guess what? Now I did too.

All my life, I'd been scared of death and dying. That's because I'd always felt that I had something to live for. The Bible speaks of this great place where everything is peaceful, and we have to work our asses off hard to get there after we leave the flesh. But this wonderful place is only promised to those who walk the straight and narrow and are unmarked. Well I've been marked, and I'm sure it was by the beast. I don't know where the triple sixes on my body are hiding, but I'm sure they're there, invisible to the naked eye. Hell, I was conceived in sin, born into a world of sin and raised in it. Why should I think I won't die in sin too?

Dog Food

I'd worked hard to follow the Good Book's Ten Commandments, but I found a hiccup with each one. The one commandment that fucks me up the most is the one that says honor thy father and thy mother. How in the fuck was I supposed to do that when I didn't know who the nigga is that I'm supposed to be honoring? Where in the Good Book was the amendment to the commandment that says: unless you don't know who your daddy is? Even with that up in the air, I still tried to do the honoring thing when it came to my mama, but that backfired when I realized she was trying to turn me into a bitch.

My faith has always been strong. I love the Lord, and I know He loves me. But He'll have to excuse me, because getting into heaven's Pearly Gates was no longer a goal of mine. Fuck the straight and narrow and my piece of the Promised Land. I'd rob, steal and kill just to enjoy my slice of heaven on this hell-ridden Earth. I didn't give a fuck if Omar was ready for what he was about to face or not, but he'd have to fight for the number one spot in the city.

What I had that Omar didn't have was book smarts, which taught me how to strategize and use logical thinking. Thinking logically, I knew this nigga had years of street smarts and the drug game under his belt. It would have been foolish of me to think I could walk in and knock him off his throne. When it came to trying to fight the way Omar was accustomed to, I only had a ten percent chance of winning. That's where strategy came in to play. I shut down all my stash spots and sent everyone that could leave the city down to Biloxi, Mississippi, with Rico to keep shit popping for me down there. Those that couldn't leave the city for days at a time went on road trips for me, and I made sure not to send them more than eight hours in any direction.

I wasn't taking myself out of business but temporarily suspending all of my transactions in Memphis and using my resources to make plays elsewhere. I wanted Omar to think he was winning the war, but in all actuality, I was using his ass like a pawn to knock out everybody else. I didn't want to fight a lot of battles with niggas I never knew just to get to the main event. My plan was to skip the season and the playoffs and head straight to the super bowl of battles. I'd let him go to war and lose causalities as I recruited and strengthened my numbers with niggas I thought could be trusted. Gutta had given me everything I needed to live the good life, making every dime I earned in the streets extra, and I didn't mind sharing. If you paid niggas well and treated them right, there was no need for them to try to take over your world. Everybody wasn't born to be a leader, and there were a lot of niggas comfortable with not taking on the responsibilities that came with leadership. Those would be the niggas I'd welcome to my team. Once the city was mine and Omar and Lord King were knocked out of the picture, I'd step down and give it to Rico. I knew my hunger to be the top man was only present as long as it was a hunger of Omar's.

I called Teresa from the bank and had her meet me at the downtown Marriott. The past month had been so hectic with moving everyone from the stash houses around to new locations and still supervising thirty people at work that I had forgotten about calling her. It took a week of calling to kiss her ass and mass text messages, making her think she was constantly on a nigga's mind, to get her to agree to meet me. I wanted to make sure everything went right. I had two bottles of Moet on ice, chocolate-covered strawberries by the whirlpool and yellow rose petals covering up everything to show that I was sorry for standing her up. I even had the petals around the toilet seat and in the tub to ensure I had given her royal treatment. I was still an engaged man in my heart and wasn't ready to move on from Bria. I was using Teresa to get a nut and to feel like I fucked a bitch that I knew Omar wanted. I felt if I got the pussy first, I was a step ahead of him. I'm sure he was only using her to get the house signed into his name. That's why he never called her when the shit didn't work out for him, but there was always a possibility he'd reach out to her again regarding the house. I might even need to use her to reach out to Omar for me. Either way, I needed her to be solidly on my team.

"Oh, boo, this shit is so nice. Are these real roses you got on everything?" Teresa asked, holding a rose petal to her nose to sniff it for authenticity.

"I told you I was sorry, and I only wanted to give you the best, baby."

She spun around in a circle like she was in a fairy tale, grasping the finer things in life at her reach. I laughed then took her by the hand, escorting her out of the room. There was no need to leave the hotel for anything. There was a five-star restaurant on the first floor and a sports bar near the lobby. After we ate and got some liquor in our system, we'd be headed right back up the elevator. The only issue I had with the hotel was that it was a smoke-free joint, which meant I'd have to go on a small detour to hit my blunt, but that was cool.

"What's good to eat here, Demarcus? All this shit don't make any sense to me."

"I don't know; it's my first time eating here."

She rolled her eyes up to the ceiling. "Nigga please! I bet you be in this bitch every weekend with a different girl. Stop fronting."

To say she worked at a bank, Teresa was ghetto as fuck. She looked the part on the outside, but everything that came from within could be labeled ghetto fabulous. I could tell by the way she looked round at our hotel room that she wasn't used to shit, but I wasn't prepared not to have an enjoyable conversation with her. Sadly, she wasn't able to hold an intellectual conversation.

"Naw, that ain't me, sweetheart. What do I need with a lot of different women who probably belong to a lot different niggas when I can put all my focus into one that's willing to put all her focus into me? I'm a one-woman type of nigga."

"Boy, you're game is on point! But for real though, I'm feeling what you said about that one woman shit. That's real shit." She laughed annoyingly, and then told the waiter she'd have the chicken and French fries which were on the kid's portion of the menu.

I didn't want to embarrass her by correcting her. Instead, I ordered for us both and played the gentleman role. Once our meal was done, we sat at the bar and watched the rest of the Memphis Grizzlies game on the big flat screen as we drank. It took a lot of probing to uncover something that I liked about Teresa besides the way her dress fit on her body. She was sexy as hell with those thin lips and slits for eyes. She had a look that probably would turn me off if she would have been skinny, but the thickness of her body complimented all of her thin features, including her razor-cut, short hairdo.

To my surprise, she was truly smart as fuck. She knew that loan, mortgage, credit, equity, and interest rate shit like the back of her hand. She was shooting off numbers and percentages left and right, and I didn't have a clue about what the fuck she was talking about, but I didn't stop her. It was my first peek at how intelligent she really was. The shit was turning me on.

"I didn't mean to talk your ear off, Demarcus. I just get excited whenever I talk about my boring-ass job. Where I'm from, nobody would ever be trusted to work in a bank or to touch people's social security numbers," she giggled.

"Yeah, you got me excited too. But don't stop, I want to know more. How did you get so good with numbers?"

She looked me in my eyes then looked away for a second and brought the contact back. "I was like you. Not the same drug, but the same hustle. I got into it to help my brother out. He wasn't the sharpest knife in the drawer when it came to that school stuff, but he knew how to get to the money, so I stepped in as his personal banker. I started off with just packaging and weighing shit out for him to free up his time. But once his right hand man got caught fucking his money over, I advanced into handling his money for him."

"Damn."

Dog Food

"Wait, before you get to damning. I'm not glorifying my past, but I learned a lot during those days. Instead of letting the shit go to waste, I flipped it into something legal. That's what makes me the best at what I do. You can learn a lot of shit that's used in life from growing up in not-so-good areas. You understand what I mean don't you?"

"Yeah, I understand you. You ready to get back up to this room?"

"Hell yeah I am, daddy!"

The entire elevator ride, I wanted to rip all her clothes off of her and hit the emergency stop button to give her some right then. The fact that she was open and honest about her past upfront turned me on. Teresa made me wish that Bria had been as forthcoming with her past, and she also made me wish she had been more like Bria. She had the looks and the smarts, and I hated to admit it, but I was missing the diva Bria had in her. I felt like a Gemini. I loved what I hated and hated what I loved. The struggle between their differences had fucked me up in a way I didn't expect. It fucked me up physically.

"Are you not feeling me? Is that why you can't get your dick hard?"

"I am feeling you. I don't know what the fuck is wrong with my shit," I said, flipping my jellied meat from one side of my thigh to the other.

Teresa wasn't accepting my response as a final answer and started kissing down my bare chest until she reached my man. She tried kissing on it for a while then sucking on him. She even went as far as slapping it across her face for whatever reason she thought that would help, but he was dead as the inventory in a morgue.

"You ain't no down-low brother are you? Because I don't do that sodony shit." She moved away from me.

"You mean sodomy, and hell naw, I don't do man pussy. This shit ain't never happened to me before, and it's pissing me off because I want to be inside of you bad as fuck right now."

That was the truth. I wanted to give it to her, but I couldn't. It's like my mind and dick had switched places. Although my mind wanted to beat her shit up, my dick felt loyal to Bria. I watched Teresa take all her clothes off and still nothing happened below my waist.

She got in the bed, turned her back to me and pressed her ass into me to spoon. "Can you hold me at least then?"

"Yeah baby, I can hold you."

Within minutes, she was sound asleep. I was left awake and horny, stroking my limp dick.

Chapter Twenty Three: Call It Tough Love

I hated to call what happened between me and Teresa a tragedy, but that's exactly what it was. As how most tragedy draws people closer together, the same happened with us. Teresa went from being a failed fuck to a best friend. She became the one person besides Rico that I could talk to about my problems. She respected my male ego by not bringing up my inadequacy when it came to pleasing her and took our friendship full throttle. I trusted her with my information, but not enough to tell her details of what was going on with me and Omar. I confessed to her that it wasn't me who walked into the bank originally, and she said after getting to know me, she could tell the difference in my and Omar's conversation. But she was still amazed at how much the two of us looked alike. Our conversations took us to Omar, went in depth about my rape charge, and even into discussing Bria. What I liked most about Teresa was that she wasn't judgmental. She seemed to take my side on everything I threw out to her. She even went as far as asking me if I wanted her to reach out to Bria for me, but I declined the offer.

"Then text her and tell her that you love her, Dee. She's a woman and not just any ol' tramp in the streets. She accepted your proposal, which means she loves you too. Yeah, you fucked up by not telling her about your past and that you were pushing work, but anger and hurt don't last forever. Trust me, boo, if she loves you, that girl has been checking her voicemail, email, and whatever else she got going on to see if you've tried to contact her. Even if it's just once a week, reach out to her to show her you still love and care about her!"

I was apprehensive about it, but I started sending Bria a text message every Monday telling her that I loved her and that I was sorry for the hurt I caused. It got to the point where I started giving her updates on me, even though I knew she'd never respond. It felt good to reach out to Bria and made the weeks go by more smoothly than it probably would without the one-sided contact. On nights when Rico and I were staking out Omar's house, I'd stare up at Adam's room, wondering what Bria was doing up there with the lights on. I liked to pretend she was up there looking at one of our pictures and missing me. Whenever I'd get lost in my thoughts of her, it was like Rico could tell and he'd remind me to stay focused on the mission at hand.

Dog Food

It took three months of us scoping out Omar's house and acting like his shadow to figure out where his big stash house was at. The muthafucka was heavily guarded, and it would take some more planning to hit it, but we knew we would. He had an old mom and pop store that had a raggedy ass house in the back of it in Frayser. By the looks of it, you'd never think they would store anything in that bitch; but after long days and nights of watching him and his workers move, we realized that it was the spot. They had niggas walking in the store and exiting through the back door to get to the house. There was a gate that allowed access to the house, but no one ever used it. Lord King and Omar wanted people to think the house was vacant and they even painted the windows all black so you couldn't tell when the lights were on inside. Getting into that bitch and finding out how many niggas were inside of it would take more investigating than running in Omar's house. I had told Rico about the tunnel Omar had dug under the house to make himself an exit when we were kids. With all the construction he had done on the house, I didn't know if that entrance still existed, but Rico was determined to find out. He and Spank decided to try and get into the house Thursday night when we had timed Omar not to arrive back to the house until after ten o'clock. I sat on the couch, chain smoking blunts until they made it back.

"We got in," Spank said, dirty as fuck from crawling under house. "But we kinda fucked up!"

"We ain't kinda do shit!" Rico chimed in.

"What do you mean by fucked up? What happened?"

Spank turned to Rico for the answer until he saw Rico wasn't going to respond. "Video surveillance. The nigga got cameras all through that bitch."

"And…" Rico added, urging Spank to continue.

"And Rico said we probably should call it off for a week, so we can plan to cut the power and bring some flashlights, but I was tired of waiting. Dee, look at how long it's taking us to make a move on the nigga. Every time y'all gas me up to think we're about to move in on him, y'all want to call the shit off. So I went inside anyways. But don't worry, they couldn't see my face. When I saw the first camera, I took off running right back to the closet, and got the fuck out."

"That's why I said we move smart, Spank. You should have listened to Rico and waited. As a matter of fact, why don't you go home and think about how you might have fucked up all these months of planning and what you plan on doing to fix the shit. All it takes is one small fuck up, and all the shit we've been doing was in vain!"

Dog Food

I opened up the door and slammed it once he was on the other side of it.

"Hey Dee, it's still early. I think we should go back and check shit out, just in case this is the last time we can get in there."

"My thoughts exactly. Let's go!"

We put on all black and stopped at the bargain store to grab some ski masks and flashlights. We made it back to the house by eight thirty, which gave us just enough time to look around and leave. Rico got out the car first and went behind the house to cut the power off. He crawled under the house with me right behind him. With the first flash of light, I noticed that Omar had torn the wall down that separated his room from mine.

"Ain't this about a bitch!" I said aloud.

"What Dee?"

"When we were younger, the nigga said he would buy the house and turn my room into a strip club. Look at that shit!"

Where my room used to sit was a small stage with two stripper poles coming out of it and connecting to the ceiling above. There were four lights pointing at the stage and a bright red curtain hanging behind it that read *Omar's Palace* in black, cursive writing. Where my bathroom used to be was a Jacuzzi with large mirrors on three of the surrounding walls. He had a large entertainment system where my bedroom door once was, and on his side of the room was a home theater with movie-style seats and a projector screen the length and width of the wall. The closet we had crawled into was still a closet, but hanging on the rails were nothing but stripper outfits, feathered wings, and leather pleasure whips. My stomach turned flips, and I was hit with the urge to throw up. As I looked at the small details I had missed when I first entered the room, Rico went to check the rest of the house.

"Aye Dee, come look at this shit!" Rico had only made it a few steps into the hall before calling me. "This nigga got a fish tank built in to the wall and filled with sharks. That muthafucka leads all the way down to the next room."

I flashed my light on the tank and this nigga had a fish tank from the floor to the ceiling with sharks the size of five-year-old kids swimming in it. Rico didn't know it, but I had seen enough. I didn't need to go check the kitchen, living room, or what used to be my mama's room to know that the nigga had turned the house my mama worked her ass off to keep up into his mini-mansion. I was furious! I wanted to pick something up and smash his fish tank wide open, but knowing him, he paid big money to have his shit reinforced like they had at the aquariums.

"Rico, let's go!"

Dog Food

Rico came down the hallway from the direction the kitchen was once in.

"We ain't even started looking for shit yet. What you mean let's go?"

"Exactly what I said."

"Man, I just found a safe in the kitchen next to the—"

"I don't give a fuck about what you found nigga, I said let's go!" I spat, ready to snap on Rico if he objected again.

"All right nigga, this is your house. You said let's go, so we're gone."

I didn't hear from Rico after that night for about a week then I got a collect call from him. He was back in jail.

"They got me in here on a bullshit violation charge, but you can get me out, Dee."

"What do I need to do? How much is your bail?"

"Fuck trying to make my bail. All you need to do is come up here and drop the charges on me. I'll be straight after that."

"Drop what charges, Rico? You speaking another language to me right now, nigga."

"It's a long-ass story."

"Well, you're in jail. You've got nothing but time to talk, nigga. Spill it!"

"Man Dee, remember I told you that the nigga had a safe in your house?"

233

"Yeah, and I also remember saying fuck what that nigga had and let's bounce."

"Right, but the muthafucka was one that I used to crack all the time, so I grabbed Spank and went back to hit it the next day—"

"What?"

"I know Dee. I fucked up, but with all the weight this nigga is pushing and all the time we've been spending trying to use your weak-ass strategies, Spank's words got the best of me, and I couldn't walk away from the shit."

"Spank in jail with you?"

"Naw, once I triggered the alarm, the nigga bounced on me."

"So, in other words, you're telling me Spank is smarter than you?"

"I know you're mad at me, but—"

"Mad ain't even the word, Rico," I interrupted him.

"If you wouldn't have been bullshittin' all these months, I wouldn't be in here in the first damn place, Dee!"

I wanted to hang up in his face and never answer another one of his calls, but Rico had been loyal to me. He helped me get out of my situation when I was locked up. I had to return the favor. In a way, he was right, but he wouldn't make me take the blame for his mistakes.

"Gutta said you had greedy ways and liked to run shit your own way, so I shouldn't be surprised you went for the safe after I told you not to. I'll take my deed and get your charges dropped."

"Thanks Dee! All you gotta say is that you gave me permission to enter the house. I told them I triggered the alarm on the safe trying to use the stove."

I cleared my throat then said, "I got you, but not until my business with Omar is finished."

"What nigga?" Rico snapped.

"You heard me. If I drop the charges, Omar will link the shit back to me and know that we are working together. I can't have you fucking shit up for me."

"Look Demarcus, I can't be waiting in here forever. If you come drop the charges, I'll just get a petty four to six month sentence for violating my probation for leaving the state. The longer it takes you to move, the longer I gotta sit."

"Well, look on the bright side nigga. You got four to six months to learn some self-discipline before I leave you in charge of this shit. I'll be up there with the paperwork as soon as this shit is done. It's still love, my nigga."

I took the lesson Gutta had taught me on tough love and applied it to Rico. I hung up the phone and blocked all collect calls from coming in. It fucked me up to do my nigga Rico like that, but I wouldn't let anything or anyone fuck my plans up, not even him.

Chapter Twenty Four: Voices From The Past

With Rico locked up, I needed to put my plans in motion faster than I had originally planned. I had Spank out here to help me get my goons together, but I needed more help from niggas I knew could get the job done. Against everything in me, I reached out to Orlando for help and he set up a meeting with me at the club we had Gutta's birthday party at in Nashville. When I walked in the VIP section, the warm smiles that greeted me the night of the party had disappeared, and I was looked at like an enemy of the state. I extended my hand in attempt to shake some of the hands of the people Orlando invited to our meeting, but no one shook it. In return, all I got was head nods and grunts.

"So what's up, Dee? What did you need to talk to me about?" Orlando asked, not sounding one bit interested in what I came to talk about. The dryness of his tone made me want to turn around and walk back out.

"I need your help."

"Help comes with a price," one of the niggas sitting to the right of Orlando announced. I later found out he was an ex-employee of Gutta's.

"Y'all can keep every dime you get and divide it up amongst each other. I'm just trying to get revenge."

Everyone sitting on the leather couches looked at each other, and then a light-skinned nigga who introduced himself as Gutta and Orlando's cousin spoke up. "How much are we looking at splitting?"

"From my researched estimate, I'm guessing close to a million dollars. Maybe even more if you include the guns and heroin you'll get."

Orlando stood to his feet and asked me to take a walk with him as the five niggas on the couch talked among themselves. Orlando took me to the men's restroom as he had done the night of Gutta's party.

"A million dollars or better on one hit? Who are you trying to get, and please don't say King David or you wasting my time."

"A nigga named Omar. You ever heard of him?"

"Omar? You mean Big O? He works for Lord King; them are good people. You started beef with Lord King?"

"My beef ain't with Lord King. It's with Omar, and Lord King has been formally warned. He's playing the background these days and letting Omar run the shots, but he has to be stopped!"

"I still don't understand why you trying to hit them niggas up."

It took longer than I expected to explain the shit to Orlando. I had to tell him that Omar was behind the stash houses being hit and my personal beef with the nigga.

"If, and I do mean if, we decide to do this with you, it ain't for your personal reasons, please know that nigga. I'll put the rest of them up on game and see what they say. Why don't you go see a little of Nashville for an hour or two, and I'll hit you up and let you know what we decide to do? If we agree, we need to hear your plan, and the bitch better be flawless."

Orlando must have thought I was the same Demarcus he met a few years ago. I was twenty-five years old now, and my world was a lot colder than it used to be. Biting my tongue was no longer necessary.

"That ain't gone work for me 'Lando, but I'll tell you what I'm willing to do. I'll go take a seat at the bar and have me a few drinks. If one of you don't come downstairs and get me in thirty minutes, forget that we even had this conversation. I know we ain't cool, and you holding a grudge against me because your brother left me his shit, but you need to know I didn't ask for it. Omar is down there taking everything your brother owns. If you feel like the shit is rightfully yours, go get it. Like I said before, anything y'all get is yours. My pockets are straight thanks to your brother."

I turned my back on the nigga like he was beneath me and headed down to the bar. For a nigga who asked for an hour or two to huddle up, he sure brought his ass downstairs to get me in fifteen minutes. I ran down the plan to the niggas and they were with it. A week from that day, Omar's life would be history.

Everything was going as planned. It was hard to track down Uncle Leroy, but when he heard he could make five hundred for not doing shit, he said, "Now that's my kind of work!"

I sent Bria a text message Monday morning when I made it to work. I wanted to let her know that this may be the last time she heard from me. I told her that after going through all the bullshit life had sent my way, she was the highlight of my time on this Earth. For the first time since I'd known her, I broke down and told her the truth about everything. I even told her that I snooped through her books under the guest room's bed. I wanted to come clean like a Catholic at confession. When I was done texting her, I called Teresa on her office phone to schedule some time to hang out Friday night. If it was going to be my last night in the flesh, I was going to spend it in some pussy. I tried to call Mr. and Mrs.

Dog Food

Roberts, but neither answered their phones. I left a message on their answering machine thanking them for everything and apologizing again for what I let happen to Bria. Maybe I was just feeling emotional, but I even told them to thank their son Adam for all the clothes they had given me when I first got out of jail. My last bit of business was to write Rico a letter that I wouldn't send off until Friday, with a copy of my deed enclosed. I told him I would be leaving him everything Gutta had blessed me with if shit didn't go my way. I made it his duty to make sure Bria never had a want in this world. I sealed his letter and placed a stamp on it as the text message indicator went off on my phone.

Why does this sound like a good bye, Demarcus?

It was Bria, and the tears swelling in my eyes almost prevented me from reading her words.

Because it might be! I got some shit I have to handle Saturday that I might not walk away from. Can I see you before then?

I didn't get a response back until Friday night, right before meeting Teresa.

No, if you want to see me, I'll meet you Monday after you let me know you're okay!

Monday ain't promised to me baby.

It is if you love me like you say you do, Demarcus!

I do love you, Bria. I love you more than I've ever loved myself. That's why I need to see you now. You won't understand, so I won't try to explain it to you. Can you meet me?

She waited an hour into to my night with Teresa to text me back.

No, I'll see you Monday. If you love me like you say you do, why would you lie to me?

I didn't know what she was accusing me of this time, but the fact she was texting back prevented me for starting an argument. *I'm sorry baby for whatever lie you feel I've told you!*

Stop playing stupid Demarcus! You know what lie you told. Love wouldn't let you keep up this charade.

I really don't know baby, please tell me so I can make it right.

Once again the text messages stopped. I was trying to put myself and Teresa in the mood when we made it to our room, and Bria must have felt the upcoming infidelity like women's intuition. *You lied about knowing and helping him!*

Baby, I swear I don't know him. If I did, I'd kill him myself. What's the niggas name?

That was her last text of the night and the start of my limpness, but this time I played it smart. Since Bria was the only person I wanted to spend my last night in the flesh with, I did. I turned off every light in the hotel room and even

Dog Food

unplugged the microwave and the alarm clock so their glow wouldn't distract me. I turned Teresa over on her stomach to prevent seeing her face, and she then became Bria. As her moans grew louder with each of my strokes, I used my hand to cover the sounds coming out of her mouth. I refused to let her moans fuck up what me and my imagination had going on, and made love to my pretend fiancée until the sun came up.

Dog Food

Chapter Twenty Five:
The Show Down

"Omar, you can't get a better deal than this. Who else do you know that is willing to sell you a twenty-two-inch rim for twenty dollars?" Uncle Leroy was at Omar's door as planned.

"What the fuck am I supposed to do with one twenty-two-inch rim, Unc?"

"Put that bitch on the front driver side of your Lexus and stunt on this niggas, nephew. Ain't nobody in Memphis riding clean like that, and if you buy it from me, I'll throw in two free car washes as a bonus. Fuck with your Unc. You know I'm a trend setter. Watch how niggas ride your dick and try to do the same."

"That shit ain't even safe. Get your smoked-out ass off my porch with that junkie shit and take the rim with you!"

That was my cue to make my way underneath the house. I told Uncle Leroy to keep that nigga at the door for seven minutes and he'd get his five hundred. When I made it to the closet's entrance to the house, I sat there listening to see if Unc still had Omar's attention.

"What about this hat, nephew? I've seen you all on my nuts every time you see a pimp like me walk up in it. You know you've always wanted it. You ain't gon' look as good as I do in it, but it'll get you some pussy. Give me two dollars and it's all yours. I'll even autograph the bitch for you. Niggas ain't gone be able to tell you nothing when you pull up in your hat, sitting on that one twenty-two-inch rim. But I'm gon' try to get you them other three rims later on tonight."

Spank texted saying Omar's stash house was wiped out and, from the looks of it, they had gotten a few million in cash and heroin. I entered the house and stood by the entertainment room door, listening to Omar talk shit to Uncle Leroy.

"I'm going to give your ass to the count of ten to get the fuck off my porch or I'm going to shoot you in yo' junkie ass, Unc."

I eased the door open and made my way down the hallway, passing the shark tank slowly. When I got halfway down the hall, Omar was standing at the beginning of it with a gun pointing at me.

"We've been waiting on you to show up."

I stopped in my tracks then was nudged forward by a gun lodged in my spine.

"Keep walking, bitch!"

I threw my hands in the air and did as I was told. Omar turned his back to me and walked into the living room where Lord King and six other niggas waited. Everyone in the room had heat in their hands. There was a chair placed in the center of the room as if they were expecting my solo visit. My mind raced on who would have told my plan to Omar, but the only person that came to mind was Uncle Leroy. If I was going to die, I felt like I should know who snitched on me at least.

"Who told you I was coming?"

Omar still had his back to me and was handing his gun to Lord King.

"You know what? I got a call from one of my workers after you arranged for my stash house to be hit. He said he was being held at gunpoint and one of the robbers wanted me to know that somebody was on their way to my house to kill me. The shit was anonymous, so once we get to the torturing session, I'm hoping you'll tell me who it was."

I knew I shouldn't have trusted Orlando. Gutta had warned me too many times not to. Omar balled up some cloth and turned around with duct tape in his hands. At the sight of me, everything he was holding hit the floor.

"Dee? Demarcus? You're the nigga behind all my grief? My own fucking blood? This shit can't be right; he's a bitch."

"Naw, you're the bitch nigga, a broke one at that!"

He searched around the room like he could get an answer from someone in it, but everybody looked as shocked as him.

"I heard you got out of jail and moved up north for a new start. Ain't that what you found out, L.K.?"

Lord King nodded his head without showing any signs that he was lying.

"Well you heard wrong then, bitch! I like how you tried to steal my house and that strip club shit added a nice touch to the place." I jumped to my feet, trying to spring on the nigga and guns from every direction pointed at me as my cell phone hit the floor.

Omar fell out laughing. "Did you really think my killers were going to let you put a hand on me? Let's see who you've been talking to." He unlocked my screen then said, "One new message from wifey. I wonder what your bitch is talking about." He fumbled with the phone. "Aw this shit right here sounds like your bitch ass in the dog house. Wifey says, 'Stop playing with me Demarcus, you know who the fuck it is!'" As he went to look through my other messages, my phone went off again. "It's wifey. She said, 'It's your cousin, Omar!' Who the fuck is this bitch?"

Like a dog in heat, I pounced on Omar and gave him three swift hits to the face. The blood from his nose shot out everywhere as the niggas pulled me off of him.

Dog Food

"You raped Bria and got her on heroin. One of y'all niggas better kill me because this nigga ain't gon' live to see another day!"

His people quickly restrained me by duct taping me to the chair. Once Omar got himself together, he gave me one to my jaw. I knew it was broken on contact.

"What are you doing with my bitch, Demarcus? That right there is enough to get you killed, but I want my money. Tell me who got it?"

It was hard for me talk, and even though Orlando had warned him about me, I would die before I helped him recover his shit.

"Bria ain't no bitch; that's my fiancée. Kill me Big O, because I ain't telling your ass shit!"

He sent another blow to the left side of my head, close to my temple. It dazed me, but it didn't knock me out.

"How is she your fiancée nigga, when she's my wife? I thought you were into raping young girls anyways? And how's your mama doing? When you get to heaven, tell the stupid bitch I said hi. One of y'all off this nigga!"

He still had my phone in hand, staring at Bria's number.

"Bria, Bria, Bria. I finally found your ass!"

I couldn't hold back the tears any longer, so I tucked my head down, closed my eyes, and started praying to the Lord for forgiveness of all my sins. I ended my prayer with a loud "Amen".

However, I still never heard any shots go off, and I guess Omar had realized the same.

"What the fuck is you hos waiting for? I said shoot the nigga!"

When I lifted my head and opened my eyes, everyone's guns in the house were pointed at Omar, but he had yet to realize it. Lord King stood up and made his way over to me.

"Are you okay, Dee?"

I shook my head yes as Omar turned to face his goons.

"Is y'all bitches slow? Point the gun at that nigga, not me!"

"Omar, did you really think I'd sit back and let you kill my only child in front of me? I've let you have your fun by whooping his ass, but enough is enough!"

Joy, pain, and all kinds of mixed emotions hit me at once. I wasn't sure if I'd heard right or not, but it sounded like Lord King had just confessed to being my father. I shot him a questioning look, but Omar took the words right out of my mouth.

"Your son? That nigga ain't your son. His mama was a ho. Any nigga over the age of fifty could be that nigga's daddy."

Lord King nodded his head at one of the men standing close to Omar. "Killa, would you do me a favor and shut that niggas mouth for me please?"

Dog Food

Like a robot, Killa reached over and popped Omar square in the mouth, making him fall to his knees from the impact.

"Dee, I'm sorry I never told you, but I promised your mama I wouldn't. She didn't approve of the lifestyle I was living. When she found out she was pregnant with you, she wanted us both to get saved, so we could raise you the right way, but I couldn't. This ain't the time or the place to be playing catch up, but I need you to make a decision. You think you can do that for me, son?"

My head was all fucked and I probably should have shaken my head no, but I nodded it up and down instead.

"Dee, what do you want me to do with Omar? Before you answer, you have to remember that he's your blood cousin. He didn't know you took over for Gutta, and he really didn't have nothing. I'll say this again to make sure you understand me, Omar had nothing to do with your rape charge at all. I can vouch for him on that. It was them greedy, dumb bitches trying to get rich. You take a minute to decide."

I looked Omar in the eyes and for the first time in our lives, I saw fear staring back at me.

"Demarcus you can have your house back man; we cousins nigga. I'm your older twin, remember? You know I just be fucking with you. I love you, nigga!"

Visions of Bria's pretty face flashed across my mind and the diary entry she wrote begging God for help made it too easy to make my decision.

"Kill him!"

Omar begged and pleaded and tried to kick out of their grasps.

"You heard the man. Killa and J.P., gag the nigga, put him in the trunk then get rid of him."

"L.K., listen to what you're saying. I've been down for you since I was sixteen. How are you just gon' kill me off that nigga's words? He didn't just rob me for everything, he robbed you too!"

"Omar, you've been trying to retire me, so you can take over for months now. Seems to me, after getting rid of you, I can retire at my own will in peace. Take his ass out of here."

Killa and J.P. finished hog tying and gagging Omar and then carried him out.

"The rest of you, we will talk later. As of right now, y'all are trespassing on my son's property!"

Without a word, everybody cleared out the house, and Lord King untaped me. I couldn't wait for us to talk, because I had so many unanswered questions. But I noticed Lord King hadn't removed all the tape, and I was still tied down.

"What the fuck were you doing here this morning, Demarcus? When you're running shit, you send folks to do your dirty work. Your ass should have never been here. That's why I sat back and let Omar give you a taste of real life

Dog Food

punishment. If this is the shit Gutta taught you, it's time I take you under my wing."

"I...I thought I'd catch him here alone. He's always by himself on Saturday mornings."

"Well, you thought wrong. And who are these niggas you trusted to rob me with? You see they turned their backs on you. What do you plan on doing about it?"

"I haven't thought about it yet," I said, not sure if Lord King was setting me up to get the information to get his money back or if this was an attempt at a father and son bonding session.

He hadn't shown me any proof that he was my father. For all I knew, Omar and the rest of his goons could be standing on the other side of the door, waiting for him to come out with the information. I decided I wouldn't answer any of his questions until I was freed.

"Untie me, pops."

"I'm not untying shit until you agree to listen to me and do what I say! As of right now, you're the only heroin dealer in the city, and you just let some other niggas fuck you out of over two million dollars that would have been yours when I retired. I'll let you free if you promise me you will let me re-teach you the ins and outs of the game, and that you'll try to get every last dime of your money back!"

The shit still didn't feel right, and he still wouldn't be trusted yet, but I said yes.

He embraced me in his arms once I was untied and promised me we'd spend every day he had remaining on this Earth together.

I didn't know what would happen as I turned the knob on the front door, but I knew once I walked out, nothing in my life would ever be the same.

The End... Or Is It?

I don't know if these niggas needed new shocks or if they had decided to hit every bump on the road, but my body was flying everywhere around the trunk. This was the final few minutes of my life, and I had to spend them getting hit by dirty gym shoes, tire irons, and whatever the fuck it was that just spilled all over my back. I wanted death to come faster than this. These niggas could have killed me first then disposed of my body afterward. The ride was so fucked up, but what made it worse were my thoughts of my bitch-ass cousin giving me my death sentence. Out of all the people I've fucked over, this nigga got the last laugh, the churchgoing mama's boy who cried about everything I'd ever done to him. I used to laugh at that shit when Uncle Leroy would say he without sin throw the first stone, and look how they let the male Virgin Mary throw his. This shit was all fucked up. Not only did the little faggot rob me for my money, but the nigga also stole my bitch. How in the fuck did that happen?

The car started slowing down until it came to a stop. I didn't know where I was, but I knew the shit was lit with bright lights. I thought I had taught Killa better than that. He knew not to do shit where a crowd could gather. As the trunk opened, I shut my eyes. Maybe if they thought I was already dead, they wouldn't put a bullet in my head.

"Wake up, nigga; we here!"

Killa said it with too much authority in his voice. He must have forgotten that just yesterday I had him vacuuming out all of my cars for me. Now the nigga wanted to flex and act all tough and shit on me because he had a gun in his hand.

"Listen up. You got two options, Omar, and I'm only going to give you one chance to answer. Option one, we can kill your ass now like Lord King said and go back to kissing his ass. Option two though, will benefit us both. We'll let you flee the state and live if you give us everything we need to knock your uncle and cousin out the picture so we can take over. I mean, we need the connect info, your cell phones, keys to all of your cars, the password to that big-ass safe in your kitchen and anything else I left out. We'll buy you a ticket to wherever the fuck you want to go as long as you promise to never bring your bitch ass back. Is that a deal?"

I nodded my head yes as fast as I could. Fuck Memphis! I didn't need Memphis to make shit happen. All I needed was a group of muthafuckas addicted to a drug to make money. Killa wasn't running shit but his dick hole. I'd stack up, and if I

Dog Food

wasn't comfortable where I was headed, then I'd come home. There ain't a nigga alive that could stop me from coming back to my city. When they untied me, we all walked into the Greyhound station together like friends.

"Good afternoon, sir. Where would you like to purchase a ticket to?"

Without a second thought, I knew exactly where I wanted to go. I wanted to be where the opportunity to make money was available, and I could get my vengeance. With a smile on my face bigger than my dick, I looked the bitch in the face and said, "Give me a one-way ticket to Detroit."

To be continued...

SUMMER 2015

DIGITAL RELEASES BY K'WAN

KWANFOYE.COM

K'WAN PRESENTS

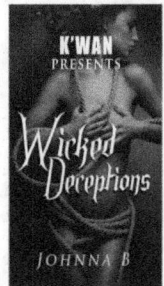

Raynesha Pittman

ORDER FORM

WRITE 2 EAT CONCEPTS
P.O. BOX 32605
MIDTOWN STATION
NEWARK, N.J. 07102

TITLE	QTY	ISBN	PRICE
GHETTO BASTARD		9780982492062	$14.95
DOG FOOD		9780982492079	$14.95

MAKE ALL CHECKS OR MONEY ORDERS PAYABLE TO:
WRITE 2 EAT CONCEPTS, LLC
TOTAL + S&H = $_____

PLEASE INCLUDE $3.95 S&H (Priority Mail)
NAME: _____
ADDRESS: _____
CITY: _____
STATE: _____   ZIP: _____
EMAIL: _____

FOR BULK ORDERS PLEASE CONTACT THE PUBLISHER
KWANFOYE.COM/WRITE-TO-EAT-CONCEPTS
WRITE2EAT2@GMAIL.COM

FREE SHIPPING
+ 10% OFF FOR PRISON ORDERS